AMANDA LEE DIXON

EXPECT
FOREVER

—PEAK VALLEY FOREVER SERIES—

Expect Forever

Amanda Lee Dixon

Copyright © 2020 by Amanda Lee Dixon

All Rights Reserved

Cover design by MaryDes
Website: www.marydes.eu

Editing Services by Silvia Curry
Website: www.silviasreading.webs.com

Expect Forever

Table of Contents

Prologue

Police sirens flare in my rear-view mirror just outside the Peak Valley city limits. I've got a six-hour drive back to Dallas, and Sheriff Warren McKnight can't let me leave without a parting shot. I have obeyed every fucking traffic regulation since arriving a few weeks ago for the Thanksgiving and Christmas holiday, and I've been pulled over half a dozen times by McKnight or one of his deputies. The prick has a giant stick up his ass.

     Getting my wallet from my back pocket, I pull out my driver's license, insurance card, gun registration, conceal and carry permit, along with my German shepherd Molly's vaccine records. It will be the same dance and pony show—they'll make me wait while they search my vehicle, then question my concealed firearm and my dog. Technically, they can't do this, but I don't say otherwise. I know it's McKnight's way of letting me know Peak Valley is his town and he calls the shots. Like father like son. His father pulled this kind of bullshit on my brothers and me back in the day.

"Eric Colson. Leaving town?" McKnight asks as he scans the inside of my truck.

"Pretty sure that's none of your business," I scoff. Molly sits up, releasing a soft growl and showing her teeth. "How will you waste my time today, McKnight? I know I wasn't speeding, and I came to a complete stop back there on Main Street."

"Thought we should have a little chat, man to man," McKnight says, putting his hands on my windowsill and leans down. A pair of cold brown eyes peer down at me. The true Warren McKnight has slithered out from behind his Mr. Nice Guy mask.

"Well, seeing as there's only one man here and I'm not wanting to chat, you might as well let me be on my way." I scratch my chin then flash him my best 'good ole boy' smile.

"Funny." McKnight's mouth twitches before he gets to the point. "Every time you come into town, you somehow drag Sarah into whatever mess you're poking your nose in and she ends up hurt or in danger. Some advice, Colson, stay away from her."

"Don't think you're in a position to be giving me advice," I say, squeezing the steering wheel tightly.

"She doesn't need your brand of trouble." McKnight shrugs, his hands white-knuckling the windowsill. He wants to hit me. I can smell his outrage, but he won't act, not with Molly in the car. He knows she'll protect me. He also knows the kind of business I'm in and won't risk getting caught doing anything nefarious. It would tarnish that shiny badge pinned to his chest.

"You think she wants your brand of wannabe hero?" I taunt, because why not? McKnight's a tool who thinks he's untouchable wearing that badge. Besides, I'm growing tired of his games. He waged war on us Colsons long ago and wants to keep it going, even if I don't live in Peak Valley anymore.

"Consider this a warning." He stands and walks away.

"You realize she lives 1500 miles away, and that she doesn't belong to either of us, right," I call out the window.

McKnight pauses but doesn't turn around. "Oh, we'll see about that," McKnight says over his shoulder, then pulls out his police-issued flashlight and breaks my taillight. Can't say I didn't see that coming. "Oh, and Colson? You'll want to get that fixed."

1
~Sarah~

One Month Later

"Your office suits you," a deep voice says that makes my body heat up and my heart race. Eric Colson. I haven't seen him since Christmas. He warmed my bed for two weeks as we reacquainted ourselves with each other. One thing Eric and I are good at is picking up where we left off, then parting ways, returning to our lives where he lives in Texas and I live in South Carolina.

But for some reason, this last time was different. Neither of us were prepared for the bubble we wrapped ourselves in to pop. I saw it in his eyes when we were about to leave. He wanted more, and so did I, but the distance scared me and ultimately, in the end, one of us would have had to make a sacrifice. It just didn't seem fair. A gamble with odds that left you both somehow at a loss.

The irony is that in high school, Eric was the boy I vowed to never date, yet he wormed his way into my heart and broke it when he insisted we part ways after we graduated. I was leaving for college, and he had to stay behind to care for his younger brother Jax. I thought we could have a long-distance relationship, but he didn't want me to wait for him. He figured out at eighteen what I'm just now starting to understand.

If only life would stop throwing us together. Some would see it as a sign. I don't know what it meant, but pretending we had an expiration date saved me some heartache—until the goodbyes were harder to do and I couldn't deny being in love with Eric any longer. I needed to put a stop to whatever this was between us.

Now he's here in South Carolina, standing in my office doorway, handsome as ever, staring at me as if I'm the only thing that can cure his addiction.

"What are you doing here?" I stand from my desk, fighting back the urge to greet him. I want to touch him to make sure he's really here. I want to kiss the hell out of him, but if I do, I'll read into him being here. And then I'll start believing in signs.

His tie is loose around his neck, the top button undone, and I bite my tongue to stop from licking my lips. Why does he have to look unbelievably gorgeous? His dress shirt showcases his muscular build. His black hair is longer than I remember, and those cool blue eyes that haunt my dreams scan me from head to toe, undressing me slowly.

"The FBI asked for a consult on the Port Pirates Motorcycle Club case they are working." He flashes a rare smile, crossing his arms and leaning against the doorjamb. "Thought I would come check out this swanky office of yours."

"FBI consult?"

"The lead witness you brought in, darlin', his intel is old. They needed more information on the key players for their case," he says nonchalantly, as if being a consult for the FBI is no big deal, but that's Eric. He always plays things down. He was never one to brag and never let success get to his head. It's why I love and hate him. He never acknowledges his true potential, yet he will do everything in his power to help others succeed.

"How long will you be consulting for them?" I ask, hesitating to step away from my desk and nearly trip when my heel snags the carpet. I'm quick to catch my balance, but the near trip has Eric pushing off the door frame and stepping fully into the office. He shuts the door behind him and stalks over to me. I don't move but watch as he comes closer.

"I'm only here for the day. I have an early flight in the morning. Thought I would see if you could show me around this town you love so much."

"I don't love this town as much as I love Peak Valley, but it does have a lot to offer. Do you want to grab something to eat?"

Bad idea . . ..

Having dinner with Eric is taking two steps backward, but I was naïve to think I could resist him. All my self-control leaves me when he's in my presence. I know how the night will end. Being together was never a problem. It's mind-blowing amazing, but when the sun comes up, he will leave and I will be lost in my feelings all over again. Will I ever be able to quit him?

"Yes, I want to eat," he says. His hands slowly slide around my hips, burning a trail of desire in their wake and short-circuiting my brain.

"What do you want to eat?" I feel my restraint slip away, leading myself down a path to more loneliness.

"I don't care what we eat," he pulls me closer, his arms wrap around my waist, and he dips his head to run his nose along my neck, "as long as I get to eat you for dessert."

*****

The front door is barely shut before Eric hoists me up and my legs wrap around his waist as he pushes me up against the wall. The kissing started when the elevator doors shut, taking us up to my apartment floor and hasn't stopped even while entering my apartment. It's a nice apartment, small but perfect for me—especially since I work long hours and spend more time working than actually living.

Eric pulls away from the wall and carries me down the entryway toward the open living room and kitchen layout. "Which way?" His husky voice, thick with desire, murmurs close to my ear.

"Through there." I point toward the barn-style sliding door behind the couch. Eric navigates around my furniture with ease. His corded muscles underneath his clothes flex, and I grow impatient, wanting to rip the cloth barrier away. No more reservations, no more worry. My thoughts are focused on Eric and the passion I've ever only experienced with him.

Eric slides the door away and drops me onto the bed with a soft thud. He follows me down, laying over the top of me, holding his weight with his arms braced around my head. There is more than just mischief in his eyes, more than just longing and desire. There is emotion in those eyes that draws me in, dares me to believe in happy endings and question everything I thought.

"Dessert first," Eric says and pushes away from me. His hands roam down my side, making a slow descent toward my thighs before reaching the hem of my skirt and hiking it up. I can't remember what underwear I put on this morning, but from the way Eric's eyes dilate into two black orbs, it must be a sexy pair.

Fingers skate slowly up my center and I jolt up, arching my back and curling my toes. It's been too long since I've been touched so intimately. Eric has been the only man I've been with in months—no, years—and I always forget how amazing he and only he can make me feel.

Our connection, our passion makes coming together mind-blowing.

Eric gently pushes on my belly, pinning me to the bed and undoing me with each featherlight pass down my center. He likes being in control in the bedroom. I never mind because he gives me exactly what I want and right now, I want him, here in my bed, in my apartment, even if it only for one night.

I lick my lips in anticipation when I feel the scrape of fabric slide down my legs. Eric hikes up my skirt before his warm breath caresses my core. My body trembles with need as I fist the comforter, waiting to feel Eric's tongue taste me.

His finger glides through my folds, spreading me open before his mouth covers my clit, licking the bundle of nerves, obliterating me in seconds. Stars dance before my eyes when Eric slides a finger deep inside me, curving it to hit just the right spot. How is it possible that only one man can make me feel this good?

"Right there," I moan, spreading my legs wider as he slides another finger in. I shouldn't be so close to falling over the edge into oblivion, but Eric does that to me. He knows exactly how to touch me and turn me on.

He relentlessly fucks me with his hand and I'm dangling over the edge, close to falling. He sucks on my clit hard when I clamp tight around his fingers and an orgasm rips through me, blurring my vision and wiping out any sense I have left as I fall apart into a million little pieces. I don't want to be put back together, not if I can feel like this for eternity.

We stay wrapped up in each other's arms for the rest of the night, exploring each other's bodies until we fall into a deep slumber. I want him to ask me to follow him. To offer to come here. Something other than denying we have a connection I know I won't find with anyone else. But he doesn't offer, and in the morning, I wake up alone, the sheets cold.

2
~Eric~

"Colson, we need to talk," Dex Traeger, my lead private investigator, says as I walk into *Colson Investigations.*

"Christ, can I walk into the office and grab a cup of coffee before my day starts?"

"Sure, but make me a priority," Traeger says as I carry my bag into my office and dump it onto my cluttered desks. I hate clutter and my team knows it. They think it's funny to leave piles of files, paperwork, receipts, and tech gear on my desk while I'm out of the office.

Colson Investigations opened its doors seven years ago—once I had learned everything I could about running my own PI business—and it has been thriving from the start. I've been lucky but honestly, I wouldn't have the success I have today if it wasn't for the guys and gal I hired. The business runs like a well-oiled machine. They're all dedicated, well-disciplined employees with a knack for pulling pranks.

I need coffee before I'm going to clean this mess up. I shouldn't have taken the first flight out of Charleston. What little sleep I got was the best damn sleep I've had in weeks, but it wasn't enough.

I head for the small break room just down the hall from my office and pass several closed doors. There are five private investigators working for me and one administrative assistant, who I think is going to retire soon. Each investigator specializes in a certain investigative area, ensuring we provide top-notch services to our clients. Some of our specialties overlap, ensuring in appropriate coverage and a reduced backlog. Speedy case closures has helped pull in more clients. I'm worried we're growing too fast, working too many cases, and if I don't start looking at expanding soon, I might risk burning out my guys.

While I walk down the hallway, I scan my investigator's offices, making sure everything looks clean and nothing is out of place that would compromise our customer's trust. I trust my guys, but I run a tight ship and demand excellence. Customers look beyond credentials and the image we reflect. The space we work out of is often a deciding factor when selecting a private investigator, and I take those criteria seriously.

"Colson, glad you're back in the office. We need to talk about the computer upgrades." Cricket catches me on my way past her office. She's our youngest PI, but a wiz with technology. I discovered her when I worked her mother's divorce and custody investigation. At only nineteen, she had evidence gathered against her father I wouldn't have known how to obtain. I offered her a job after the investigation was complete, and she has become one of my greatest assets. "I need your signature so I can get the orders placed."

"Can you put something on my calendar so we can review what you plan to purchase?" I ask while still walking.

"Already done, just need you to accept the meeting notice," she says, keeping pace with me. "I need you to talk to Griffin, too. He hates change, and I have to upgrade his accounting software, even if he doesn't like the new interface. I have vulnerabilities I need to patch."

"Have you told him the risks?"

"Yes, and he is stalling until you give the go ahead on the computer upgrades." Cricket holds her coffee mug out for me to fill.

"I assume you left the proposal on my desk with all the other crap?"

"I would never do such a thing." She smiles and shakes her head. "Thanks for the coffee."

"Can we talk now?" Traeger asks, ruffling Cricket's hair as she walks by, receiving a smack to his shoulder. All the guys see Cricket as their little sister—full of innocence and mischief. She's petite yet lively, with doe eyes and an unassuming smile. While they respect her abilities, they are also extremely protective of her. I pity any guy she finally gives her attention to—he will be cross-examined, interrogated, and thoroughly investigated before any of us approve.

"Yeah, follow me into my office. You can help clean up the mess you made," I say before we leave the break room.

"I would never make a mess of your office. You should talk to Jane . . . she's always putting stuff in your office."

"You're a filthy liar, Traeger!" Jane, my receptionist, hollers from the front desk.

"You're hard of hearing, Jane. I said you are always keeping this place in check while Colson is out." Traeger winks at her then closes my office door behind us.

"I get the feeling this isn't about a case you're working on."

"No, it isn't," Traeger says seriously, his teasing smile gone as he takes a seat in front of my desk. Traeger has worked for me the longest, signing on a year after I started my business. His restlessness lately has concerned me. I know he's been chomping at the bit for more responsibilities, but I haven't had much more to give him. Leaving him in charge is the least I can offer. "I think you know I've been wanting to take on more around here . . .."

"And you do great acting as my delegate while I'm out of the office." I nod, taking a seat and moving my bag underneath my desk.

"Since you put me in charge as your delegate, I've been thinking about starting my own firm." I can't say I'm surprised. I left the PI firm that trained me to branch out, offering more services and having more autonomy. When I simply nod, he continues, "Starting out on my own means I won't have the luxuries I have now."

"This is true. *Colson Investigations* has been operating for seven years, and we've lost clients preferring a PI with more than ten years' experience."

"Exactly." Traeger nods, steepling his fingers. "Have you thought about opening another location? A sister location that offers the same services, but also expanding on the service offerings, bringing in more investigators and covering more territory?"

"I have." I don't elaborate. I thought about opening a second location in Charleston, South Carolina, but that's as far as I've got with the thinking. I haven't told anyone about it because it would be me operating out of the South Carolina office, leaving headquarters behind. My team is settled here in Texas, rooted to the area with family and friends. I'm the only one not tied to this place. "Do you have a second location in mind?"

"I don't have a location in mind, but I wanted to discuss the possibilities of letting me buy into your business and become a co-owner. I would run one location; you can have this location and together, we operate under the same umbrella."

"You do know this isn't something we can just shake on and jump headfirst into. We would have to research locations, hire new personnel, draft service packages, and market the new location," I say, watching him closely. Traeger isn't one to make rash decisions. I know he's been considering this for some time, and so have I. I need to come to a decision whether I want to move to South Carolina, bringing me closer to Sarah, or expand here in Texas, effectively cutting off this thing Sarah and I have tangled ourselves in.

I don't want to cut things off between Sarah and I, but she hasn't given me any indication that she wants anything other than a hook-up. A part of me is hoping she will give me a clue, something that will help me make a decision.

"I understand, and frankly, there will be a lot I would need to learn from you before I take on a co-owner role." Traeger breaks into my thoughts. I roll my shoulders to loosen the tension that has formed since leaving Sarah this morning.

"I doubt there is much more I can teach you. Give me some time to think about this and do some research. I like the plan, but logistically, there is a lot that needs to be considered."

"Thank you." Traeger stands and extends his hand to me. I stand and shake it.

"How were things while I was gone?"

"Everything ran smoothly," he says and smiles proudly. "I proposed to Lisa. She said yes."

"I've only been gone a few days . . .. When did this happen?"

"You were gone over Valentine's Day." Traeger raises his brow.

Shit! My little detour to see Sarah was on Valentine's Day? I glance at my desk calendar to be sure and my stomach twists. If I wanted to see a clue, I just blew it.

"Lisa has been hinting pretty hard that she expected a ring when I didn't propose over Christmas and New Year's," Traeger says.

"Seems a bit sudden," I mutter, half listening as I think of ways to rectify my shitty actions.

"Yeah maybe," he winces, "but it made her happy."

I shoot him a confused look and when he looks away, I quickly congratulate him, not meaning to sound like an asshole. Traeger hasn't been dating Lisa long and she wasn't someone I saw Traeger getting serious with. She has big expensive dreams, and the salary PIs make would never meet the demands she has.

"Thanks," Traeger says stiffly before he changes the subject. "How was the FBI consult?"

"Long." I sigh taking a seat. "They have a pretty solid case but not enough witnesses to testify."

"Always seems to be the case." Traeger shrugs. "Come find me when you think more on what we discussed."

"I will." I nod as my phone rings and Traeger quietly leaves my office, shutting the door behind him. "Eric Colson."

"Hey Eric, it's Luke," my older brother says when I answer.

"I know it's you Luke. Caller ID." I roll my eyes. "What do you want?"

"You stored my contact info? Ahh, so you *do* love me." Luke chuckles into the phone.

"Yeah, yeah," I groan, rolling my eyes then sit up with an idea. "Hey, when you fuck things up with Amber, how do you fix it?"

"Why do you assume I fuck things up with Amber?"

"It isn't an assumption. You've been fucking things up with her since high school." I smile into the phone as I sit back in my chair and prop my legs up on the desk.

"Whatever, asshole," he grumbles.

"Seriously, Luke, what do you do?"

"Tell me who you fucked up with and I'll share my secrets." I can hear the smile in his voice. *Bastard.*

"No," I say flatly. I'm not telling him about Sarah. I know if I did, Luke would then tell Amber, who would immediately call her sister, demanding details and possibly ruining any opportunities I have left to keep Sarah and me connected.

"Suit yourself. You're a PI, I'm sure you can figure it out on your own."

I pinch the bridge of my nose. "Fuck you."

"So . . . you fucked up with Sarah," Luke says, and I groan.

"Amber tell you that?"

"No, but only one woman has ever frustrated you like this, so it isn't hard to figure out." Luke chuckles. "What'd you do?"

I drop my head and rub the back of my neck. "Nothing, just drop it."

"Amber is holding onto hope that the two of you will figure something out and move back to Peak Valley."

"I'm not moving back to Peak Valley. Besides, even if I did, what would I do? Come work for you? Sounds boring, no offense."

"I wouldn't call life in Peak Valley boring. I've had enough drama to last me a lifetime."

"True, Peak Valley has become a magnet for danger lately."

"Hopefully things will settle down soon," Luke mutters into the phone, sounding tense.

"Any word on Henry's case yet?"

"Yeah, he pleaded not guilty. There's going to be a trial. Sarah said we'd all be called to testify."

My brother's new fiancée Amber was almost killed over the Christmas holiday by her ex-husband Henry. He plans to try his luck with a jury despite all the evidence stacked against him.

"I can't say that I'm surprised. When is the trial set for? I need to make sure I'm not working any cases that could be impacted by my absence."

I knew the moment Henry was arrested he would deny any involvement. I also knew both Sarah and I would have to testify. We were both there when the hitman broke into Amber's house. I was grazed by a stray bullet and Molly almost died trying to protect us. I want to see the bastard burn.

"May fifteenth. Three months away." He sighs. "Seems too far away. Amber doesn't want to set a date for the wedding until the trial ends, but I'm growing impatient."

"Speedy trial is an oxymoron," I mumble as I write down the trial date.

"Sarah expects the trial to take a week, maybe two. I hate that Amber has to go through this." I can hear the concern in Luke's voice.

"How are the kids handling things?"

"Surprisingly well. They both seem relieved to be honest. Amber has them in counseling, and we learned the kids never spent much time with their father. He was always working or not in town. I think I'm more upset about the whole thing than Amber is."

"She's probably relieved and doesn't have anything to worry about. The kids going to their dad's house was probably more upsetting to her knowing they weren't being cared for the way a father should care for them," I add, doodling around the trial date.

"Yeah, Burns said the same thing." Luke sighs. Burns is the only man who gave a damn about my brothers and me. He practically raised us after our mom died and our dad checked out. He's a man of wisdom and a royal pain in the ass. I'm glad Luke has him to lean on while he and Amber deal with Henry's bullshit trial.

"Luke? Is something bothering you?" I question, sensing there is more he wanted to talk to me about than just Henry's trial.

"What makes you think something is bothering me?" he shoots back defensively.

"You have that deer in headlights sound to you."

"Nothing gets past you, does it?" He chuckles and I can picture that goofy grimace he gets whenever he's hesitant.

"What can I say? I'm good at what I do."

"Well, it's annoying."

"I have a gift." I laugh, leaning back in my chair and staring out my office window. "Now tell me what's bothering you."

"With Henry out of the picture, I'm worried I'm going to screw them up. The kids, I mean . . ." Luke confesses, the sound of a hand running down his face muffling his voice.

"Seriously? You're worried about messing up the kids?" I laugh out loud, shaking my head. Luke would give his right hand if it spared Emily and Matt the smallest amount of pain. "Luke, you have nothing to worry about. You didn't screw us up." We didn't have the most conventional upbringing. We lost our mother due to a car accident when we were young. It drove our father to drink his life away, and Luke, being the oldest, was responsible for us. Until I had to kiss my future away to care for Jax while Luke was in the military and Clint was at trade school in Kansas City.

"Clint and you seem well-adjusted. Jax, on the other hand, is—"

"Wild and unpredictable?"

"Yeah."

"He's outgrowing it, though. I heard he bought *Benny's Bar*. Plans to turn it into a brewery. Never thought I would see him settle in one spot."

"It's nice having him back in Peak Valley. Wish you were here, too." Hope permeates through the phone.

"Never going to happen, brother."

He laughs. "Famous last words."

"Nothing will convince me to return to Peak Valley." I chuckle, dropping my feet from my desk. "I need to get to work, Luke. Don't you have work to do? Clint's house isn't going to build itself."

"Yeah, yeah. Don't work too hard, brother. And give Clint and Jax a call sometime. They miss you."

"Yeah, yeah," I mimic. "I'll come up early for the trial. That make you happy?"

"It would," Luke says seriously, and I'm tempted to tell him that I miss him and my brothers, even Burns, but I don't want to give him more hope. Since his return to Peak Valley, he has hinted at wanting to reunite us all again. I wasn't lying when I said there wasn't anything that would convince me to move back to Peak Valley. The town holds nothing but bad memories and an enemy who wouldn't hesitate to make my life miserable.

Expect Forever

3
~Sarah~

Two Months Later . . ..

"Pregnant? That can't be true. It's been months since . . .."

    "Do you remember when your last period was?" Dr. Louis Brown asks with a trace of sympathy as she looks through my chart.

    This can't be happening.

    I came to the see Dr. Brown after feeling nauseous for the last few weeks. I just thought it was a stomach bug I couldn't shake. I was supposed to get a B12 shot, not a pregnancy diagnosis.

Is pregnancy actually a diagnosis, though? Or is it considered a condition?

"I haven't paid attention. I'll have to check my phone." I barely choke out as I reach for my phone. Eric's visit was in February. I can't remember when I had my last period as I scroll through my calendar app. "I think January seventh, but the last time I was with someone . . . was February fourteenth."

"We go off of when your last menstrual cycle started, which puts you at about ten weeks," she says with her head down, scribbling in my chart.

"Ten weeks," I say out loud, still processing. "I'm pregnant." I run a hand through my hair. I'm going to have a baby. I never gave much thought to having a baby. It wasn't something I wanted to dwell on. Thinking about having a baby seemed out of reach, and I didn't want to hope for something I wasn't sure was ever a possibility for me—not with the hours I work and the life I live.

"The father?"

I lift my gaze to her. "Excuse me?"

"The father, I assume is your significant other."

"Oh, um . . .."

"I'll keep it blank." The doctor nods her head as her finger moves to the next line on the chart.

"Eric Colson," I respond, not sure if I should be insulted or embarrassed with her questioning.

"I'm writing you a prescription for prenatal vitamins. You'll need to start them immediately. Take them, they will help you. Do you need names of an OBGYN?"

"Right, I'm going to need an OBGYN," I murmur.

"The nausea is normal and can last until around fourteen weeks. If it gets severe, call me. You're still young, so I don't anticipate any complications, but you should schedule an appointment as soon as you decide on an OBGYN. Do you have any questions?" she asks, looking away from my chart.

"Oh, um . . .."

"I take it this wasn't planned." Dr. Brown is moving so quickly through the questions. Doesn't she see that I'm trying to wrap my head around this?

"No."

"Might I suggestion taking some time to think about this? You have options—"

"Options?" I cut her off. *Options?*

She folds her hands in her lap and gives me a sympathetic smile. "I only mean to give you all the information available to you."

I swallow, shaking my head. "Thank you, doctor, but I'm keeping my baby." I sit up straighter, shaking off my shock as a protectiveness turns my backbone to steel.

"Okay. I'll leave some pamphlets at the desk. You can get dressed and remember, call if the nausea gets worse." She smiles before she stands and leaves the room.

Looking down at the paper gown, I place my hands over my stomach. I may not have planned this but without hesitation, without any doubt, I know I want this baby. How could I not?

*****

"Mom?"

"Sarah! What a pleasant surprise." My mom's voice soothes some of the tension in my shoulders. After filling my prescription, I came home, wanting nothing more than to hear my mom's voice. I miss home. I miss a lot of things.

"Shouldn't you be with a client or nose deep in case files? You normally call after seven."

"I took the afternoon off," I say, rubbing my shoulder.

"Oh? Are you not feeling well?"

"Something like that . . .."

"Sarah, you don't sound like yourself. Is everything okay?" I can hear the concern in her voice.

"Yeah, just a little overwhelmed at the moment." I sigh over the lump in my throat. My emotions are turning me into a punching bag. A jab of excitement, a right hook of fear, knocked with joy, and sliced open by loneliness. It's hard to pinpoint exactly what I am feeling.

"Honey, tell me what's going on. Maybe I can help." Before today I would have rolled my eyes at her coddling. My mom was an amazing mom. The best. I can only hope to be half the mother she is.

"I'm pregnant." It slips out, followed by a gasp from me or my mother, I don't know. Neither of say anything for a moment and I pull my phone from me ear, looking at the screen to see if she hung up. "Mom?"

"I'm here."

I close my eyes and brace my hand against the couch. "Say something."

"I'm not sure you'll want to hear what I have to say," she says softly, but it might as well have been a punch to the gut.

I wince and bite my thumbnail. "Just say it."

"Sarah . . .."

"Mom," I groan, letting my head fall back against the couch cushion, tears blurring my vision.

"I'm so thrilled. *A baby!* Oh, Sarah, this is wonderful news. Did you just find out? You must have just found out," she gushes, her words streaming together almost incoherently.

Relief replaces the pit that was forming in my stomach and I smile. "Yes, I just found out. I thought I had a stomach bug."

"I was sick as a dog with you for the first two months, and with Amber, too."

"Hopefully I will be lucky, and it will end soon." I manage a laugh. "Mom, can you keep this to yourself for a while?"

"Yes. Yes, of course. I won't even tell your father until you give me the green light. How far along are you?" So many questions.

"Ten weeks."

"Oh . . ." she trails off with a touch of surprise. "Are you seeing someone new?"

"No." I roll my eyes. I never told her about Eric's visit. I only told my sister Amber and my best friend Dawn. *Dawn*. She's pregnant, too. Our babies will be cousins.

"So . . .."

"Eric is the father," I confirm.

"So, you two . . .."

"He was in town for work. It was a short trip."

"I bet he'll be so excited. He's held a torch for you since you two were young. Have you told him?" Ah, and there it is, the million-dollar question.

I suck in a deep breath before exhaling, wishing I could dance around this but what is the point? "I haven't told him. You're the first person I've told."

"Are you worried about telling him?" *Oh, Mother, you know me so well.*

"I-I don't know how to tell him." I sigh, running a hand through my hair. "I should do it in person, right? This kind of news isn't something you share over the phone, right?"

"Well, you're sharing it over the phone with me . . .." I can hear the smile in her voice.

"It's different with you, Mom. Besides . . . I don't know what I'm going to do."

"Going to do?"

"Having a baby changes everything. I can't exactly raise it in my small one-bedroom apartment while working eighty-plus hours a week. I have to make some major changes."

"What kind of changes do you plan to make?"

"I don't know yet. I know I want to be a mom who isn't working all the time, missing major life events while someone else raises my baby." I stand from the couch and pace my living room, still nibbling on my thumb nail. "If I cut back on my caseload, I have no chance of making partner at the firm and honestly, that thought doesn't bother me. I'm excited about motherhood, but I have no idea what I'm going to do next."

"It will be difficult not having a support system around to help," my mom adds, and I pause my pacing.

"Yeah, not having you or dad around to help will be hard," I say, twirling a strand of hair around my finger.

"I could come visit before the birth and help you out. I'm sure your father wouldn't mind coming to visit again, either. He's been looking up new places to visit."

"I guess . . .."

"We'll have to stay at a hotel though since your apartment is so small . . .. Unless you move into a new place before then? Do you think Eric will move to Charleston?" she rambles off and I fall onto the couch ready to cry. So, *so* many questions I have to answer. How am I supposed to do this alone?

"No, Mom, I don't think Eric will move to Charleston. His life is in Dallas." I try not to sound like I'm on the verge of tears.

"You could always move back home," she suggests with hope dripping in her tone.

"And do what?" I rub my eyes. "I would need a job to support myself and my baby."

"Larry Rutledge is wanting to retire. You should call him about taking over his law firm."

"Isn't his son taking over the law firm?"

"His son opened his own law firm in Kansas City, and Larry's wife is itching to move out there to be closer to her grandbabies."

"Hmm . . .."

"And if you move back to Peak Valley, you'll have me and your dad, as well as Dawn and

Amber to help you. You could have it all, Sarah. You could be a mom and have a career."

"You make it sound so easy," I say, laying down on the couch and looking up at the ceiling, not ready to think about how perfect her plan sounds.

"Because it *will* be easy. It's always easier when you have your family close by and in your corner."

"I'll think about it," I say, though the idea is already taking root as plans begin to formulate.

"Oh good! I'll send you Larry's number. Promise me you'll call him."

"I will, Mom." I smile as tears stream down my cheek, excitement and hope blossoming in my chest.

4
~Eric~

"Janet! Come look! I got the jackwagon on the FaceTime," Burns yells when I answer his call. "I can see his ugly mug."

"Burns I can hear you," I groan, pinching the bridge of my nose. Why did I answer his call?

"You can?"

"I can see you, too."

"Janet he can see me, too!" Burns looks over his shoulder, then points down at the phone. "Come look."

"Of course, he can see you. You're FaceTiming him," Miss Janet says, coming to sit next to Burns. "Hello, Eric. You look tired."

"I'm exhausted. Picked up a missing person case and want to close it out before I head to Peak Valley for Henry's trail," I say, rolling my shoulders.

"When do you think that will be?" Burns asks, moving the phone closer to his face and giving me clear line of sight up his nose. "Look, Janet had me wax my nose hairs. Look clean up there? I can't tell."

"Burns, stop that. He doesn't want to see up your nose." Miss Janet swats Burns' shoulder and pushes the phone away from his face.

"Thanks, Miss Janet." I wink at her with a smirk. She's by far the best thing to happen to Burns. He needed a woman to smooth out his sharp edges. "I not sure when I'll be into town. The trial is three weeks away, and I need to wrap this case up before I can head up there."

"Luke said you would come up a little early," Miss Janet says with a tentative smile. "Sarah mentioned you might be able to help with a problem my friend Hattie has."

"Sarah?"

"Janet's friend Hattie was swindled out of her retirement. Sarah said you might be able to look into it when you come up."

"Sarah's in town?" I ask, perking up. I haven't spoken to her since my visit in February, but a day doesn't go by that I don't think about her. I came up with a dozen different reasons to call her, pulling her number up daily but never actually calling her. Everything I want to say won't change the fact that we live states away.

"Yep. Spoke to her . . .. What day was that? Saturday when we went over to help her move?" Burns says, looking over at Janet.

"Yes, Saturday, but don't go telling people you helped. You sat on your tush and watched Clint and Luke do all the heavy lifting." Miss Janet gives Burns a pointed stare.

"I was taking photos. Sarah may need them for insurance purposes."

Miss Janet rolls her eyes. "You were trying to embarrass those poor boys."

"It's payback for all the hell raising they did growing up. Did you know they once—"

"What do you mean you helped Sarah move?" I cut in before Burns could launch into one of the many stories he has on my brothers and me. Every year they get more exaggerated.

"Oh . . .. You didn't know she moved back to Peak Valley?" Janet asks surprised, her wrinkles more pronounced across her brow.

47

"She's taking over Larry Rutledge's law firm. Got herself a nice little townhouse not far from us," Burns says, pointing in the direction Sarah's townhouse must be.

"Hmm." I press my lips together, biting back a swear on the tip of my tongue. Sarah moved back to Peak Valley, and I'm finding out from *Burns*. How did I not know this?

Because you didn't call her, dummy.

"I'm sorry, dear, we thought you knew," Miss Janet says, covering her mouth and looking guilty.

"I didn't."

Burns scrunches his brows together. "You two not talking anymore?"

"How was your friend Hattie swindled?" I ask, changing the subject and running a hand over my face. Now isn't the time to talk about Sarah's sudden move, especially with Burns and Miss Janet.

"Right. Hattie . . .. Her new man friend stole all her money. Sarah said she can't help since Hattie gave all her money to him," Burns explains, animatedly waving the phone around in frustration.

"Gave him her money?"

"She loaned him the money to help him pay for his cancer treatments and when she didn't have any more money to give, he stopped answering her calls," Miss Janet explains with a frown. She takes the phone from Burns and holds it steady.

"Do you know the man?"

"No, she met him on a romance website. He was supposed to finish his cancer treatments, then move to the *Peak Valley Retirement Community* Hattie is living at, but she has to move in with her daughter Melissa now."

I rub my eyes. "I see."

"Will you look into it?" Miss Janet asks, looking hopeful and I internally cringe. Romance scams like this happen all the time. Usually the money they stole is never recovered, and the scammer almost always gets away with it.

"Send me Hattie's contact information. I'll have my cyber forensic investigator, Cricket, gather evidence before I head up. Don't make any promises to your friend. These cases don't always end the way we want."

"What kind of asshole steals an old lady's money? She's got nothin' left." Burn glares into the phone.

"A lot of times the scammer is operating in another country. Let my investigator look into this, but it isn't likely she will get her money back. Cricket has worked several of these cases. She's always able to track the scammer, but if they are operating out of another country, convictions are nearly impossible."

"That's not good." Burns looks at Miss Janet.

"I should wrap up this case in a day or two, then I'll head to Peak Valley."

"Thank you, Eric. Get some sleep, dear. You work too much," Miss Janet says with a sympathetic smile.

Burns nods. "Listen to her, Eric. Janet knows best."

"I will. See you soon." I wave and end the FaceTime. I lean back in my chair and look down at the spec sheet for a building in Charleston. It was supposed to be where I opened a second location. I picked the building for its close proximity to Sarah's office and apartment. Picking up the piece of paper, I crumble it and toss it into the trash.

Amanda Lee Dixon

5
~Sarah~

"Wow, this place is—"

"Dated?" I cut Amber off when she walks into my new office. It's a temporary office until Larry Rutledge retires and I officially take over the firm. Then I will take over his office with its better view and private bathroom.

So many remodeling ideas swirl in my head. Fortunately for me, my soon-to-be brother-in-law is giving me the family discount when he finishes Clint and Dawn's house. It won't be extravagant, but more modern as I don't make the money I use to, not as a small-town lawyer.

"It's very smoke pipe and leather in here," Dawn adds looking around at the floor-to-ceiling bookshelves with rows upon rows of law books. "Your desk is bigger than my car."

"It's not that big." I roll my eyes but she's right. The beast of a desk is all ornate dark wood and glossy finish, complete with swirled carvings decorating the edges. My computer looks foreign on top of it, to modern for the décor.

Amber looks down at her scrubs and laughs. "I'm so underdressed for this office."

"It is a bit pretentious." I shrug, shouldering my purse and grabbing my phone. "Ready?"

"Yes, I have been craving chocolate," Dawn says as we file out of my office. I wave at Larry, who is packing up to leave as well—a good sign. When we first spoke, I made sure the work hours wouldn't keep me in the office night and day. He assured me business was good and rarely was he late for dinner.

The crazy hours I used to work were self-imposed but mostly, I took on a heavy caseload to help fast-track my career and make partner. I had big dreams, but not once since I made the semi-impulsive decision to move back to Peak Valley have I regretted it. Motherhood wasn't exactly in my life plan, but now that it is, my career, while still important, isn't what I live for. The little bean

in my belly has been consuming my thoughts—
well, whenever they aren't consumed by thoughts
of Eric.

I may feel completely out of my element
heading down this path, but I'm excited with every
step I take. At night I shop for baby clothes and
look up ideas for the nursery I'm setting up in my
new townhouse. It keeps me busy and helps me
not dwell on the guilt I have for not telling Eric
about the pregnancy. I plan to, I just can't bring
myself to make the call yet.

He should be arriving here in Peak Valley
soon for Henry's trial, and I get more nervous with
each passing day. I have no idea how he will react
to the news. I also fear he will be pissed about my
move. Eric hasn't made it a secret that he wants
nothing to do with Peak Valley and raising our
child here will likely upset him. But then again,
being alone without my family raising our child in
Charleston didn't feel right, either. Being here in
Peak Valley feels right.

"Do you miss Charleston now that you've
settled in?" Dawn asks as we head down Main
Street toward *Sugar and Sweet*. Dawn is a transplant
from Charleston, having moved here almost a year
ago. I relocated her to Peak Valley when her ex's
motorcycle gang was hellbent on hurting her for

information. Now she's married to Eric's older brother Clint and pregnant with his baby—another reason why moving back to Peak Valley was so appealing. We were good friends when she lived in Charleston and having another pregnant woman to talk to will help with all the crazy changes I'm experiencing.

"Actually no. Surprising, right?"

"Not really. Peak Valley has everything you need and no traffic. What more could you ask for?" She smiles at me.

"How's the morning sickness? Getting any better?" Amber asks after several moments of silence.

"Not too bad anymore. I get a little nauseous after lunch, but the ginger tea you suggested helps."

Sugar and Sweet is mostly empty when we arrive with only a few teenage girls sitting in a corner giggling over something on their phones. I was hoping it would be empty, free of the town gossips, so I can ask them for advice on how I can tell Eric the news. I'm not ready for the town to know before Eric does.

We quickly place our orders and find a seat in the middle of the bakery. "So, how has work been? Are you still excited to take over Larry's firm?" Amber asks over her coffee.

"Yes. So excited. I made the right choice; I feel it in my gut. I have more time and my stress has dropped drastically, but I do worry I'm becoming addicted to online shopping."

"Enjoy it while you have it. Once the baby is here, you will have your hands full," Amber says then winks at Dawn. "Have you spoken to Eric yet? You haven't said a word about how he's handling the whole situation."

"About that . . .." I clear my throat not missing the glance Dawn and Amber share. "You haven't said anything to Clint and Luke, right?"

"No, but they know something is up. Clint thinks your move here means Eric is coming back, and I have no idea what to say when he asks me what I think." Dawn grimaces. "I'm not sure I'm going to be able to deflect much longer. Have you even told Eric? You would think he'd have told his brothers by now."

I swallow and look away from the two. "I haven't told him yet."

"What?" Amber chokes on her coffee. "Sarah!"

"I know!" I grumble, covering my face.

Dawn leans in close, searching my face for answers as she whisper-hisses, "Why haven't you told him?"

"I want to tell him in person." I try to sound confident with a little shrug. "I will tell him when he gets here for Henry's trial. This isn't something you share over the phone. A greater conversation needs to take place and we need to develop a plan. It has to be done in person."

"Does he even know you moved here?" Amber asks in a hushed whisper. I don't know why the two are whispering. We are practically alone in the bakery.

"I don't know . . .."

"I get why you're waiting to tell him," Dawn says with a small frown, still watching me over her tea. "But he's not going to be happy. Are you prepared for that?"

"Honestly? No." I sigh looking down and at my belly. My boobs are bigger, but I haven't seen much change in my stomach. If anything, I look bloated. According to the pregnancy books I've been reading, I will be bursting at the seams before I know it.

"Hey, don't worry. We have your back." Amber reaches across the table and squeezes my hand. "It's a complicated situation. I doubt you can please everyone, but what is important is that you are happy."

"I know he's going to be mad I waited so long to tell him, but he didn't call after he left in February. I'm not sure how he will react to it. I need to see his reaction and I need to hear in person what he plans to do."

"Are you worried about how he will react?"

"I'm terrified. What if he doesn't want to help or be involved?"

"I can't image Eric not helping," Dawn says and glances at Amber for agreement. "Besides, he's always grumpy and angry. I doubt you'll notice a difference."

Amber nods in agreement. "Eric is definitely in a permanent state of grumpiness, but he will step up. Behind that thick skin of his, he's a sweetheart."

"He isn't going to be happy about raising the baby in Peak Valley," I add with a frown.

"No, but he'll understand why you moved here, especially when he realizes he won't be around to help all the time."

"You don't think he will try to convince you to move to Dallas?" Dawn bites her lip.

"I'm not moving to Dallas," I say matter-of-factly. "I won't have a support system there, either."

"Well, honey, Eric will be in town soon. He's staying with us before we head to Kansas City for the trial. Do you want us there when you tell him?" Amber asks.

"No, I need to tell him alone."

"We're here for you. Just let us know how we can help." Dawn squeezes my hand. She doesn't know how relieved her words make me feel.

Eric and I may not see eye to eye when it comes to where I raise our baby, but at least I have my family.

"Enough about me." I shake my head. "How is your blog, Colson Cooking, doing?"

"It's going well." Dawn smiles brightly, putting her cup of tea down. "I'm surprised at how many people have visited the blog."

"Your recipes are so simple and easy, but I still can't cook as well as you." Amber laughs.

"I read your blog, but I haven't tried a recipe yet. I'm hopeless in the kitchen," I fire back. "Maybe I'll give it a try now that I have all this free time on my hands."

"I can help, just say when," Dawn says and Amber and I look at each other before laughing. "What?"

"I think you are about to have your hands full." I smile. "But I appreciate your willingness to help me." Then I glance at Amber. "Are you ready for Henry's trial?"

"Yes." Amber exhales. "I'm not surprised Henry's claiming innocence but at the same time, I can't believe the nerve he has."

"He's a narcist. In his mind, he probably believes he did nothing wrong. I'll be happy to see him behind bars," I say over my cup of tea. "The kids are handling things well."

"I'm shocked." Amber's shoulders droop. "I don't know if I should be relieved or worried that I'm missing something."

"They are doing good because you and Luke shower them with love. They never received that kind of love from Henry. They aren't missing something they never had." Dawn rubs Amber's shoulder.

"Yeah, I hope you're right." Amber smiles at Dawn and pats her hand. "We have too much drama in our lives."

Truer words could not have been said.

Expect Forever

6
~Eric~

Sarah looks out of place in her new office. It's an office decorated for an old man, not a polished, sophisticated woman. I pictured her office to be more modern with a touch of femineity to it.

She hasn't noticed me at the door yet, and I'm not exactly sure what to say to her. I never called her after we hooked up in February, but I should have. I wanted to, but every time I was about to, I'd remember how she said goodbye over Christmas. Sarah wasn't interested in a relationship, and I convinced myself that I was doing us both a favor by not calling—just like I did back in high school.

Sarah had big dreams in high school. Dreams that took her away from Peak Valley and I couldn't follow her. So, I ended our relationship. I should have followed her when I was able to leave Peak Valley, but I didn't. I had no idea what I was going to do with my life, and she had a plan for hers. I didn't want to disrupt that, and I didn't want to find her happy with someone else, so I went south when I should have gone east.

Watching her now, buried in a mountain of papers, I wonder if I should have called. If I said all the things I wanted to say, maybe she wouldn't have moved to this town full of bad memories.

"Hey, Sarah." I step into her office toward that gaudy desk she's sitting behind, watching her head fly up with a touch of fear in her eyes. It catches me off guard and stops me in my tracks.

"Eric," she says my name on a gasp. "I didn't expect you in town so early . . .. The trial isn't for another two weeks."

"Burns asked me to come up early, and let me tell you how surprised I was to hear you moved here." I tilt my head at her, running my thumb along my lower lip.

She nods, pressing her lips together. "I should have told you."

"Why didn't you?" I take a step, then another, watching her scan her eyes over me. She backs her chair from the desk as I come around it and sit on the edge of her desk. Her hands shake as she bites her lip. Something isn't right. She isn't telling me something.

"I had a lot on my mind . . .." She nibbles on her lip before looking up at the clock on her wall. When those emerald eyes of hers swivel back toward me, it's like a sucker punch to my gut with the mixture of emotion they hold. "We need to talk, Eric. Do you have some time later tonight to meet? I have a client coming in soon."

"No," I lie, narrowing my eyes at her. It isn't exactly a lie, but I did agree to meet with Hattie Smithson and Burns later this afternoon to go over her case.

"Okay." She bobs her head. "Can we meet tomorrow? It's important that we talk soon." The hair on the back of my neck raises and I scan her from head to toe. There is something different about her, but I can't place my finger on it.

"What's going on, Sarah? You move to Peak Valley out of nowhere, you can barely look at me, and you want to *talk*. Just say whatever it is you have to say." I don't want to schedule any damn appointments with her; I just want to hear her tell me she thinks we need to end whatever it is we have going on. If you can even label what we have.

"Eric, it isn't that simple. We should really sit down and talk." She pinches the bridge of her nose in frustration. "Please, can we talk later?"

"No," I say through clenched teeth. I know I'm an asshole, but I'm not a patient man.

"Eric . . .."

"Just say it," I growl, not meaning for it to come out so harsh, but I don't have time to obsess over what she has to say—and I *will* obsess over it.

"I'm pregnant."

What?

"Excuse me?"

"I'm pregnant," she says a little louder, straightening her stance and lifting her chin a little. It's the first time she's looked me in the eye.

Sarah's pregnant.

"I know I'm early, but I brought a pizza from *Carlos' Pizzeria*," Warren McKnight calls as he walks into Sarah's office. My temper flares, tinting my vision with a hazy red as I clench my fists. "Oh. Am I interrupting?"

"Client?" I arch a brow at Sarah, who looks panicked and all at once, everything clicks into place. McKnight made his move, and now she's pregnant with his baby.

"No, I mean yes . . . he is a client. Eric, can we please continue this conversation later?" She leans into me, talking quietly.

"Should I wait outside?" McKnight thumbs over his shoulder as a playful smile stretches across the asshole's face.

"Yes," Sarah cries out.

I should have called her.

"I was just leaving."

"Are you sure? There's enough here for you." McKnight smirks at me. I clench my fists before glancing at Sarah, who is silently pleading at me.

McKnight warned me that he wanted Sarah. Her move to Peak Valley made his warning a consuming thought, but I never thought Sarah would give him a chance. I thought we had something deeper. Now she's pregnant with *fucking* McKnight's baby and any hope I had disappears.

"Enjoy your lunch," I snap and leave the office, ignoring Sarah as she calls after me.

God, I hate Peak Valley.

*****

"What's with the scowl?" Burns asks as I drive us to the *Peak Valley Retirement Community*.

"I always scowl," I grunt, not taking my eyes off the road.

"You have your *I'm mad* scowl on your face. What's eating you?" Burns pushes. He has a knack for reading me, even when I don't want him to.

"I'm fine."

"I've known you almost your whole life. I know when you aren't fine. You're pissed off, so spill, you jackwagon," Burns says in his animated way. He's become more animated to hide the shaking in his hands, which is something I need to talk to Clint about.

"Fine, old man, I'm pissed off. You happy?" I groan, hitting the blinker to turn into the *Peak Valley Retirement Community*.

"What's eating you?"

"I don't want to talk about it," I grumble, knowing he won't let this go but fortunately, I park my truck next to the curb leading to Hattie Smithson's home.

"You never want to talk about it," he huffs, crossing his arms over his chest and not making a move to get out of the truck.

"C'mon, old man, we have work to do," I say as I turn the truck off.

Burns shifts to face me and points a finger at me. "I know you don't like coming home. Peak Valley reminds you of all the losses you endured, but there were a lot of good memories, too. Don't forget the good, Eric. We *miss* you."

Burns searches my face with a look of worry. The old man is more preceptive than I care to admit. After leaving Peak Valley, I rarely returned until recently. It was a reminder of the shitty childhood my brothers and I had, but he isn't wrong that there were a lot of good memories, too. Wreaking havoc on Burns in particular.

"See." He jabs a crooked finger into my shoulder with that goofy grin of his. "Remember that time we tried to convince Jax he was a sleepwalker and we moved his sleeping butt around the house?"

"Yeah, I remember." I chuckle, unable to stop the smile from spreading across my face. Jax was baffled for weeks.

"Remember when you and Sarah made a fake birth certificate for Clint on his sixteenth birthday? He thought he had to wait another four months to get his driver's license."

"I forgot about that one," I murmur, remembering Sarah and I working on creating a near perfect fake birth certificate. We had just started dating but even then, I knew she was the one.

Thinking about Sarah only reminds me of her and McKnight. How they will be prancing around Peak Valley as a happy family very soon. Burns was right; I do have some good memories of Peak Valley, but all the really good ones were with Sarah.

"C'mon, Burns. We have work to do." My smile fades and I climb out of my truck, ignoring Burns' grumbling. "Who's that?" I nod my head toward the boy trimming the bushes next to Hattie's home.

"That's Dale Hurlburt's son. Dale's the director of the retirement community," Burns answers, eyeing the boy suspiciously. "Do you think Dale could behind the scam?"

"It's too early to tell, but I'll check out the staff."

Hattie comes to the front door before we have a chance to knock and waves us in, leading us through the almost empty ground-level apartment.

"Thank you so much for coming. My daughter is in here," she says, shuffling to a small kitchen table. "Melissa, this is the private investigator I told you about."

"Eric Colson," I say, extending my hand.

"Nice to meet you." She shakes my hand, then gathers a folder stuffed with paperwork. "Hattie mentioned you are from Peak Valley."

"Born and breed." Burns nods, taking a seat at the table.

"I'm based in Dallas, Texas now."

"Have you worked a scam like this before?" she asks, hesitating before she hands over the folder of paperwork.

"I have." I take the folder and flip through the bank statements, emails, and printed screenshots of text messages. "Is this all the messages between the two of you?"

"I had her screenshot a lot of the text messages and save several pictures of him from the companion site. It's all stored on this," Melissa answers for Hattie and hands me a small USB drive.

"Were there any social media accounts you used that he was on?" I ask, putting the folder on the coffee table and taking out a notepad.

"We were on Facebook, but I didn't understand it. We mostly texted," Hattie says, wringing her hands.

"The companion site is how you met?"

She nods her head, looking uncomfortable with shame in her eyes. "Yes, we talked for several weeks before he asked me if we could communicate off the site."

"I know this must be hard going through these details with me, but you should know you didn't do anything wrong. I don't want you to feel ashamed. Scammers like this," I glance at the profile they printed off, "Hector Evans . . . they break down your defenses so they can manipulate you. They play on your emotions and take whatever they can. You aren't the first person to be scammed this way and unfortunately, you won't be the last. Coming forward is very brave. Not many people come forward and more people get hurt. I want to stop this person from hurting others. With your help, we can put a stop to him."

Hattie's eyes fill with tears as I speak. She nods before pulling a tissue from her pocket and wipes her nose. "Where do we begin?" she asks with more confidence in her voice.

"Let's start with you telling me a little bit about Hector."

"Well, he told me he was a widow, lost his wife about ten years ago. I lost my husband five years ago, and we bonded over the pain." She covers her mouth and looks at Melissa. "I bet he never lost his wife, did he?"

"Did you ever speak to Hector on the phone?" I ask, changing the subject. I'm sure the scammer posing as Hector learned she was a widow and created a fictional tale of loss to manipulate her and build her trust. Commonality brings people together but unfortunately, it can be used to bring your guard down, too.

"Hector said he was hard of hearing and that speaking on the phone was difficult for him. He wore hearing aids." Hattie sniffs, wiping her nose with a tissue. Her daughter reaches over and squeezes her hand. It's good that Hattie has a support system—she's going to need it to get through this.

"While you two were communicating, where did he say he was from?" Burns asks through clenched teeth. I give Burns a pointed stare. I appreciate his desire to help, but I need

Hattie to stay calm and not shut down before I can help her.

"He said he moved to Kansas City to be closer to his brother, who passed away a few years ago. Before that he lived in St. Lewis. He and his wife didn't have any children, just nieces and nephews, none of which he was close with. He often told me how lonely he felt."

"When did you first send Hector money?" I ask, still writing down Hattie's statement.

"He told me he was diagnosed with cancer but couldn't afford the treatments because his Medicaid wouldn't cover all of it," Hattie explains as she leans forward and opens the folder. "He even sent me the claim for the treatments."

I take the paperwork she hands me and glance through it. On the surface the document looks legitimate, but my years of experience can see its falsehood.

"Did you pay the amount he needed for the treatment?" I ask before handing the document back to Hattie.

"Yes," she says, putting the paperwork back inside the folder before pulling another slip of paper out. "Here is the Western Union receipt."

I take the receipt and glance at the location where the money was sent to, surprised to see it say Kansas City. "Did he ask you to check the box to pick up the money without ID?"

"Yes. He said he doesn't drive anymore and no longer has a driver's license." Hattie's cheeks grow red with embarrassment.

"Mom, it's okay. You didn't know," Melissa softly assures her mother.

I give her a reassuring smile. "Did you always send money through Western Union?"

"Yes."

"And always to Kansas City?"

"No, the rest were sent to Wichita where Hector had his surgery," she says as she shuffles through more paperwork. "He went to stay in Wichita while he participated in an experimental trial. I sent him money to move there for the duration of his treatment. Once his treatment was complete, he was going to move here to Peak Valley."

"When did Hector stop responding to you?" I ask, placing the paperwork back in the folder.

"After his treatments were complete in Wichita. He told me he didn't have enough money to move to Peak Valley since his house was still on the market. I told him I didn't have any more money to give him. He didn't respond after I sent that text. I tried reaching him several times, even called him, but it went to voicemail. I called the hospital where he was getting his treatments, but they said they couldn't give me any information on a patient."

"How long ago was this?" I ask, closing my notepad and putting it back inside my jacket pocket.

"We last spoke two months ago," Hattie shares, glancing at Melissa. "How much will your services cost?"

"Don't worry about my service fees, but I want to be completely transparent with you two. I will use all the tools I have to locate this person so justice can be served, but getting the money you lost won't happen quickly, if it happens at all."

Melissa and Hattie share a glance before tears slide down Hattie's face. "I'm sorry," Hattie says to her daughter. "I feel like such a burden."

"You aren't a burden, Mom. You have nothing to apologize for." Melissa leans over and hugs Hattie. I wish I could do more than just locate the bastard who did this to them.

*****

"That was kind of you," Burns says as we pull out of the Peak Valley Retirement Community. "Hattie doesn't have two nickels to rub together."

"It's nothing," I grunt, accelerating down Main Street toward Burns' home.

"You're a good man, Eric." Burns pats my shoulder. "A jackwagon sometimes, but a good man."

Sirens flare as we pass the corner of Main and 3rd and a cop car pulls up behind me. I swear under my breath.

"What the hell?" Burns says, looking over his shoulder. "Were you speedin'?"

"No," I hiss as I pull over. "Leave your seatbelt on and don't say a word."

"You in trouble with the law?"

"No. McKnight knows I'm in town," I growl, pulling my wallet from my back pocket.

"Oh, well then, maybe you should let me do the talking."

"Let me handle this." I roll my window down as Sheriff Warren McKnight leans down. "My taillights work and I wasn't speeding, so what piece of unwanted advice do you plan bestow on me today, sheriff?"

"Always a pleasure, Colson." McKnight shrugs. "Are you in town for the trial?"

"You know I am. Just say what you want to say, McKnight. I have shit to do," I spit out, clenching the steering wheel.

"Do we have a problem here?" Burns asks, pointing between the two of us.

"No problem." McKnight smiles at Burns and rubs his jaw. "Just want to make sure Colson here doesn't bring trouble to Sarah."

"Sarah?" Burns asks wide-eyed before leaning close. "Your Sarah?"

"Burns . . .." I send him a warning glare.

"What? I didn't know you two were having a pissing war over Sarah. Does she know?"

"No pissing war, right, Colson?" McKnight eyes me with that fake cool manner of his. Sarah's confession from earlier is still fresh in my mind. She was mine. Every fiber in my being wants to fight for Sarah, even if she is pregnant with McKnight's baby.

"Right," I spit out and look away so I don't let the words I want to say escape my lips. "Are we done here?"

"We're done," McKnight says before he glares and walks away.

"I see some things never change," Burns grumbles, looking as grumpy as I feel.

"Drop it, Burns," I say pulling back onto Main Street.

"You're not going to let him move in on your girl, are you?"

"She isn't my girl," I growl, pushing the speed limit.

"Since when?"

"Since she came back to Peak Valley."

Expect Forever

7
~Sarah~

"What do you mean he walked out?" Dawn asks with a furrowed brow. It has been two days since Eric's surprise visit, and he hasn't returned any of my calls or texts. Granted, I didn't plan to tell him about our baby that way, but ignoring me . . .?

"I told him I was pregnant, and he walked out," I repeat, tears sting the back of my nose. I was never one to cry over hurt feelings. I would feel the pain, then put together a plan to move past it, but apparently, pregnancy has given me an endless supply of tears.

"That doesn't seem like something Eric would do," Amber says, looking baffled as she takes a seat at the island next to me. We are at

Dawn's apartment trying one of Dawn's recipes for her blog while Clint works in the shop below. I needed to get out of the house, so when Dawn asked if I wanted to try her chocolate brownie recipe for the blog, I couldn't say no.

I'm not used to having so much time on my hands. I've cleaned my townhouse, I've continued to buy things I don't need, and binged watched so many shows I used to never have the time to do. All this time has been wonderful, but thoughts of Eric and his abrupt departure after telling him about the pregnancy consume my thoughts. The only thing that seems to help is keeping busy, but even that is becoming ineffective.

"Tell us everything that happened," Dawn says, putting down her fork and giving me her full attention. "Leave nothing out."

"He surprised me at work, but I had a client coming so I told him we needed to talk . . .."

"Uh-oh," Dawn murmurs.

"What?"

"Oh C'mon, Sarah, everyone knows when you say, 'we need to talk,' it's usually followed with bad news." Amber scoffs. "The poor guy probably went broody and intense like all the Colson men do."

"He did." I close my eyes and shake my head before opening them and running my hands through my hair.

"Let me guess, he demanded you tell him or he wouldn't leave." Amber smirks at me.

"He demanded I tell him." I nodded. "I knew if he stayed, he would get pissed when Warren stopped by."

"Wait. Why did McKnight stop by?" Amber scrunches her nose. She and Luke aren't fans of Warren after his treatment of Luke when Amber was attacked by the hitman her ex-husband had hired. I get their irritation, but he was just following protocol.

"His mom isn't doing well, and he wanted to know what he should do." I sigh. "I thought he was bringing his mother but instead, he showed up early with lunch."

"And Eric was there?" Dawn asks wide-eyed.

"Yeah, he showed up literally right after I told Eric I was pregnant. I need to hire a front desk receptionist."

"I bet Eric walked out because McKnight was there. You should call him." Amber smiles before she grabs her fork and takes a bite of her brownie.

"I *did*! He isn't returning my calls or texts. I . . . I think I'm going to have to do this alone," I confess, the idea more frightening now that I've said it out loud. I know I'm capable of caring for my baby, but I saw how hard it was for Amber all those years being a single parent.

"You aren't alone. You have us," Dawn says and gives me second helping of her brownie. I give her a watery smile before taking a giant bite, hoping the chocolate therapy will take away my unshed tears.

"Do you want me to try to talk to him? He hasn't really been around, and I think he's avoiding me . . . which kind of makes sense now." Amber grimaces.

"No, if he doesn't want to be involved, I'm not going to force him."

"You should still hold him accountable for the care of the baby," she says, annoyed. "It's not right for him to just abandon you and the baby."

"I rather him not be involved than force him to be accountable. This way I have more rights to our baby. Besides, I don't need his help."

"You can't just avoid him for the rest of your life," Dawn says quietly. "Amber is going to marry his brother. I'm married to his brother. You two will cross paths eventually, and then what?"

"I thought about that and I think it's best if I just . . . not be around when he's going to be around." I lift my chin. I had thought about the implications bringing up this baby in a family closely connected to Eric. I know what it will cost them, what it will cost me, but it isn't like I have a choice.

"No!" Amber cries out. I flinch when she drops her fork, which clatters loudly against the plate.

"Amber, please try to understand. It's better this way. It would be weird if I hold him accountable when he clearly doesn't want to be a father and then on top of that, force him to see us."

"He's probably not going to come around anymore," Dawn adds, looking sad. "The guys rarely talked before Clint and I started dating. They just started spending more time together, and Jax is back in Peak Valley."

"Eric will disappear," Amber adds.

"I think you're right." I nod, a tear slipping down my cheek. "And I'm sorry for that, but I have to think about my baby."

"I can't believe you are going to let him get away with this," Amber fumes and I can't say I don't get her anger. I've tried to be angry at Eric but all I really feel is sad. Sad he won't see this baby as a blessing, and what I had secretly hoped for as an opportunity for us to be together.

"I plan to try to tell him again. He can't avoid me at Henry's trial, but I'm not going to chase after him, either."

"I'm sorry you have to go through this." Dawn stands and moves to hug me.

"I'm sorry too, even if I do think you need to kick Eric's behind for being a fart knocker," Amber says, standing and hugging me, reminding me that I made the right decision by coming home and starting over.

8
~Eric~

"What's up, boss?" Cricket, my computer forensic investigator, greets after one ring. "Are you missing me already?"

I chuckle into the phone as I send her an email. "I need you to do some digging. I picked up a case a few days ago. An elderly woman was scammed out of her savings."

"Romance scam?"

"Yeah, but I think the scammer is local," I share as I scan through the evidence I've gathered for a third time.

"Local scammer? You don't think it's a family member, do you?" Cricket asks, clicking away on her computer.

"I don't think it's a family member, but I'm not ruling it out, either," I share, glancing at the background checks I did on Hattie's family. Nothing out of the ordinary popped up there. One daughter, a few grandkids, and none of them have ever been in trouble with the law, but it isn't unheard of, especially when someone gets desperate. Still, my gut tells me that Hattie's family isn't involved.

"Give me the rundown. What do you want me to look for?"

"The scammer used a burner phone before tossing it or shutting it off. It last pinged in the town over, River Bend, a few weeks ago. But she sent money to Kansas City and Wichita, and both cities are a few hours away. I think the scammer may reside in River Bend or Peak Valley but travels to Kansas City and Wichita to pick up the money."

"I'm looking through the details you sent. The emails were sent via an untraceable service. He's smart. I don't have much here to work on. What are you wanting me to do?"

"If the scammer is local, I have a feeling he may be scamming others in the retirement community—preying on the elderly and the lonely. I found his Facebook profile. Can you investigate and see if you can't uncover any information? Anything that would identify him or see if there are other victims."

"Sure thing, boss," Cricket says, clicking away.

"And no backdoor shit, Cricket. If we catch this guy, I want him charged, and we both know your illegal hacking won't hold up in court," I say sternly so she understands the importance the information she's trying to obtain.

"I'm not an *idiot,* Eric. I know when to be ethical about my hacking skills."

"Debatable . . .."

"Any bastard who screws a lonely widow out of her savings deserves to be locked up. I want to see this guy go down. I'll do everything by the book. Promise."

"Thanks, Cricket." I exhale a sigh. "How's Traeger handling everything?"

"He's grumpy. His new *fiancée* seems to think now that he's going to be sharing the boss title, they can have a bigger budget for the wedding, but he's holding down the fort."

"How is everything else going? Are you taking good care of Molly for me?"

"Molly is warming my feet as we speak," Cricket says, and I can hear her smile. "It's quiet here. Holden is working out of town; Zayne is setting up a security system for a super-secret client and hasn't been around, and Griffin is still a pain in the ass. We are all good, but you are missed."

"Griffin is a pain in the ass because you push his buttons." I rub my eyes and lean back against the headboard. I've been laying low at Luke's house, keeping myself busy and avoiding Amber. I've been thinking about getting a hotel room, but I'm not sure how to explain that to Luke. We will be leaving for Kansas City in a few days for Henry's trial, and avoiding Sarah will be impossible once we're there. I can only hope the trial is quick. The faster I get out of Peak Valley, the better. "How much time do you need to look into things?"

"I should have some information to you in a week if I don't find much, two tops. If the guy isn't local, you know we won't have any success getting any of the woman's money back, right?"

"Yeah, I know. I already told her it wasn't likely and that she should reach out to a support group to help accept what had happened. She was pretty devasted. I told her it happens more often than she knew and that she shouldn't feel ashamed. Scammers learn how to strip away defenses."

"How'd she take the news?" Cricket whispers, almost afraid to ask.

"Honestly, I thought she might have a heart attack. I hate that part of the job." I grimace, the woman's devasted face replaying in my head.

"Damn," Cricket murmurs.

"Alright, I better let you go."

"Later, boss." Cricket hangs up and I toss my phone onto the bed.

I shut the lid to my laptop when I hear a soft knock on the door. "Come in."

"Hi, Uncle Eric," Emily, Amber's youngest daughter, says as she and her puppy Elfie come into the guestroom I'm staying in. "Do you want to see Elfie's new trick?"

"Sure," I say smiling. She's Amber's twin and has Luke wrapped around her pinky finger. If I'm being honest, there isn't anything I wouldn't do for the cutie.

"I taught her kisses," she says, getting on her knees in front of the puppy I gave her for Christmas. I gave her older brother Matt a puppy too, earning me the favorite uncle title.

"Kisses?"

"Yeah, watch." She wiggles excitedly then looks at Elfie. "Give me kisses." Elfie pounces on Emily, licking her face and eliciting loud giggles that brings a smile to my face.

"Emily?" Amber calls from down the hall.

"In here, Mommy!" Emily giggles from the floor as her puppy continues to pepper her face with kisses.

"What have I told you about pestering Eric?" Amber comes around the corner with an apologetic smile.

"It's fine." I stand from the bed to help Emily get out from under Elfie.

"Dinner will be ready soon," Amber says, but hesitates. "Are you joining us?"

I tilt my head, eyeing her. It dawns on me that she must know Sarah is pregnant. How wouldn't she? The two sisters have always been close. A mixture of emotion assaults me, betrayal being the most dominant. Amber and Luke are not fans of McKnight, but Luke hasn't said a thing to me about the pregnancy. This is the kind of thing that he would have brought up.

I'm about to decline dinner when Emily grabs my hand. "C'mon, Uncle Eric, you can sit next to me."

"Emily, will you go wash your hands and give Eric and me a moment?" Amber says in her mom voice. I wonder if Sarah will have that same mom voice. If she has a little girl, will she look like Sarah?

"Okay," she says and rushes out of the room. She only has one speed, fast and furious. Jax use to be like that when he was a kid, too.

Amber watches her leave before she turns her attention to me. "We really like having you around, Eric . . .. I hope you know that."

I cross my arms, not interested in beating around the bush. "Does Luke know?"

"Know?"

"About Sarah being pregnant," I say through clenched teeth.

"No," she says with a sad smile. "She wanted to wait until she told you."

I nod and look away. "We should go eat before the food gets cold."

Amber watches me for a second before she turns away, leaving me with my thoughts. I need to get the hell out of here.

Expect Forever

9
~Sarah~

Henry's trial starts tomorrow, and the two-hour trip to Kansas City will be too taxing on everyone, so we rented hotel rooms for the week. If we're lucky, the testimonies will only take a week. The case is pretty cut and dry, but Henry's lawyer is calling half a dozen character witnesses.

There is too much evidence against him not to return a guilty verdict, but when the jury is bombarded with irrelevant testimonies swearing Henry doesn't have it in him to hire a hitman, you can only hope the jury sees past the bullshit.

I can only hope for Amber and Luke's sake that it will end quickly. They don't need this stress in their lives. They should be planning a wedding, not taking time off work to watch a guilty man try to convince a jury he's innocent.

Amber told me Eric is sharing a hotel room with Jax and getting him alone to speak to him will be tricky, especially with all our family and friends around.

I just need a quick, quiet moment with him. I'll tell him my plan, offer him an out, and we will part ways—just like we always do. The last time he didn't even say goodbye. I don't think he will say goodbye this time, either.

Still, I can't believe that Eric will walk away. I tell myself he will, but I can't believe it. I pictured Eric being surprised, confused, and based on the way he loves my niece and nephew, I hoped he would be happy.

I'm ready for the day to end as I gather my files and shove them into my purse. My feet hurt, I'm starving, and I'm beyond exhausted. Logically, I know cooking up a baby would be tiring, but my body feels like it ran a marathon most days. Dawn makes it look easy and she's farther along in her pregnancy, and I swear the baby in her belly is going to be a giant like her husband Clint.

"Heading out?" Larry Rutledge asks as I lock up my office.

"Yes. Let's hope I'm only out for a week."

"Take your time and get some rest. The office will be here waiting when you get back." He smiles as he walks me to the front door.

"I will. See you later." I wave as I leave the office. The spring air is refreshing with only a slight breeze.

My pants feel tight as I walk toward my car. I need to invest in maternity clothes, but I've been stalling. Maternity clothes will broadcast to everyone that I'm pregnant, and I'm just not ready to broadcast my bundle of joy until . . . well, until Eric and I part ways.

"Sarah!" a deep voice calls from behind me. Warren McKnight jogs toward me, his cruiser parked just up the street. It's the second time he's stopped by to see me. "I was hoping to catch you before you left."

"Well, you caught me." I sigh, not wanting to stand in these heels any longer than necessary. I know he's just being friendly, but this seems too convenient.

"Doing okay? You look tired." He smiles, stepping a little too close for comfort.

"I'm exhausted," I say, holding back an eye roll. I'm not normally this impatient, but I think I've entered the swollen feet phase of my pregnancy and these heels are pitching off all circulation in my toes. "What can I do for you, sheriff?"

"I've told you, call me Warren."

"Warren, how can I help you?" This time I do roll my eyes.

"I wanted to see if you had a ride to the trial," he says, shoving his hands into his pockets and eyeing me from head to toe.

"I'm riding up with Amber and Luke."

"I thought so, but I wanted to offer anyway."

"Thanks, I appreciate it, but I'm sticking close to Amber. She's handling everything pretty well, but I want her to feel supported." I give a friendly smile and take a small step back. "Whatever happened to you and Lily James?" I blurt out, feeling awkward by his closeness.

"Lily James?" Warren repeats, and his smile fades, replaced with a stone-cold glare. "Haven't thought of her in years."

"You two were pretty close back in high school. I always thought you two would be married with a ton of children running around you."

"She ran off right after graduation. Haven't seen or spoken to her since," he says quietly. Apparently, I struck a chord bringing her up. She was his high school girlfriend, and they were quite the couple back in the day.

"Shame, you two would have had beautiful babies," I say when Eric rounds the corner and heads toward Warren and me. His head is down and his shoulders are hunched. He looks pissed off, but it doesn't stop me from taking a step in his direction. "Excuse me, Warren."

I sidestep Warren, wincing when my heels pitch my toes. I have to get to Eric before he walks away—this may be my only chance to talk to him alone. When Eric's head comes up and he spots me, I pick up the pace, ignoring the way his eyes narrow into two angry slits.

He looks ready to bolt. "Eric, please wait," I call out and he glares over my shoulder. I don't doubt Warren is still standing where I left him. I'm almost out of breath when I reach him. "I . . . I need to talk with you."

"I don't think there is anything left for us to talk about," Eric growls, not looking me in the eye. That cuts deep, making it even harder to breathe.

"You don't think there is anything left for us to talk about?" I repeat, just to be sure I heard him correctly.

Eric glances at me and a flicker of hurt crosses his face before he straightens to his full height. "I think it's best if we just part ways."

"Part ways?" I repeat like a damn parrot. I can't believe this, but it came directly out of his mouth.

"McKnight's waiting for you." Eric nods his head toward Warren, then turns and walks away. He's made his choice, whether I want to believe it or not.

Stunned, I watch him walk away with tears in my eyes as the one man I have ever loved breaks my heart all over again.

10
~Eric~

Did I step into the Twilight Zone? I mean, I know Henry's trial was going to be an emotional rollercoaster for Amber, but I didn't expect her to give me the cold shoulder. Not after our conversation a week ago. Even Dawn is refusing to speak with me.

What the hell am I missing?

This whole week has been hell. I spent the last week sharing a hotel with Jax, who's barely a functioning adult and the biggest slob I've ever met. The internet is spotty, and the hours of testimony have been gurling.

I gave my testimony at yesterday. I recounted the events that left Luke and Amber's house riddled with bullet holes. I expected it to be an hour of questioning, but the cross examination was brutal—questioning my tactics, even questioning whether my dog Molly was truly hurt by Henry's hired hitman. Henry's lawyer was ruthless. I was pissed and exhausted, and I spent my time drinking the rest of the night alone while everyone went out for dinner. So far, I've been able to avoid dinners by claiming that I was working. Avoiding everyone has been surprisingly easy, but with everyone's stress levels at an all-time high, I don't think they've noticed my avoidance . . . or maybe they just don't care.

I was proud of Amber when she bravely gave her testimony. She described her fear, the shock of learning her ex-husband wanted her dead, and the terror she felt knowing he had her children. Not once did she waver under scrutiny. She was simply amazing. I wanted to tell her that, but one cold glare from her kept me at bay.

Sarah's testimony didn't take as long; being a lawyer, I think they knew she wouldn't be easily flustered. Despite her short testimony, I couldn't take my eyes off her. I knew it was the last time I could stare at her unabashed. Take in those intoxicating emerald eyes, admire the glow she radiates. Her growing stomach is starting to become visible underneath her clothes. Pregnancy looks good on her. During the testimony, her hair framed her face and I wanted nothing more than to brush it behind her ear.

She refused to look at me. I shouldn't want her to look at me, but during her testimony, I wanted nothing more than one glance my way. Just one glance.

McKnight's presence in the courtroom compounded my ever-growing bad mood. He wasn't even called to give testimony—he was just there for Sarah.

Why she chose him eludes me. I didn't take the threat seriously when McKnight first told me to back off all those months ago. I found it funny that he thought he even had a chance at staking a claim. Sarah has never been interested in him; at least, if she was, I never saw it. They were friendly but that's all it ever was.

Until you didn't call her.

They hardly appear to be a couple, especially since Sarah is always skirting away from McKnight's advances. I'm sure she's trying not to rub it in my face, but it's only a matter of time before they announce an engagement and everyone learns about the baby. I just hope I'm long gone before that happens.

"Henry, you told the defense you knew Arnold Toppler, the man behind attacking your ex-wife," Henry's attorney asks the asshole on the stand testifying.

"I wouldn't say I knew him. I met him once, and it was before I turned him in for insurance fraud." Henry smiles at the jury as if he's some sort of hero.

"So, Arnold Toppler had a reason to be upset with you?"

"Yes, I believe he was upset with me for turning him in, and when he was caught, he lied in hopes of working a deal," Henry shares, continuing to address the jury.

"This is bullshit," Jax whispers in my ear.

"He's playing the jury," I whisper back.

"Thank you, Henry. No further questions," Henry's lawyer says to the judge and turns to take his seat.

"Henry, did you call the police when you turned Arnold Toppler in for insurance fraud?" the prosecuting lawyer asks.

"I denied him his insurance claim," Henry says, his smile faltering just a little.

"You didn't report him to the police?"

"N-no . . . it's not procedure," Henry stutters.

"Do you have the denied insurance claim?"

"I'm sure my secretary can get that for you." Henry swallows.

"That's funny, we asked her for the denied claim, and she couldn't provide us with it. Is it possible you never denied his claim because there was no claim?"

"There was a claim. I assure you, I denied the claim," Henry tries to reassure but there isn't an ounce of smugness on his face.

"So, you believe Arnold decided to punish you for denying his claim, but why would he go after your ex-wife? Why not your current wife?"

"I can't answer that."

"Can you answer why you texted Arnold Toppler asking for proof of your ex-wife's murder?"

"Objection!" the defense lawyer shouts as he stands from his chair.

"Overruled," the judge answers back and flicks his gaze to Henry. "Answer the question."

"I never asked Arnold for evidence of any murder. I thought I was asking for evidence that his claim wasn't fraudulent."

The bastard has an answer for everything.

"And when he sent you a picture of your lifeless ex-wife brutally murdered, you didn't think to call the police?"

"I didn't look at my phone after that," Henry responds.

"But you did respond with a time and location to meet you," the prosecuting attorney adds.

"I don't believe I did," Henry answers, looking worried.

"Then let me refresh your memory." The prosecuting attorney grabs a file from the table and hands it to Henry. "This is your text log from your phone. Can you start reading from line twenty-seven?"

Henry looks at his lawyer. "Do I have to?"

"Yes. Line twenty-seven."

"Meet me at Dave n' Buster's at two p.m. and you'll get your money."

"Thank you, Henry." The prosecuting attorney takes the file from Henry.

"I didn't send that text," Henry cuts in.

"But you were at Dave n' Buster's at two p.m."

"Yes, but I didn't pay Arnold to murder Amber. I would never do th—"

"Enough!" the judge interrupts Henry.

"Thank you, no further question, Your Honor." The prosecuting attorney turns away from Henry and smiles at Amber.

I don't pay attention to the judge as he tells Henry he can step down. I only watch the jury, scanning their faces for a hint that they didn't believe Henry's lies.

"I thought that would never end," Jax says when the judge releases us for the day. "Closing arguments are tomorrow, and then it's over?"

"The jury has to reach a verdict," I say as we head out of the courtroom. Amber and Dawn file out ahead of us with Sarah between them. I squirm past the women and head toward the parking garage. I can't stand one more minute of the frostiness coming off them.

"I don't know if you've noticed, but the women aren't happy with you," Jax says close on my heels.

"I've noticed."

"What'd you do?"

"I don't know."

"Hey, wait a sec . . ." Jax says, putting a hand on my shoulder to stop me. "Are you going to try to fix it?"

"Yo, jackwagons!" Burns calls down the hall, shuffling toward us. "Where you two going?"

I pinch the bridge of my nose and sigh. "Heading back to the hotel."

"But we're planning dinner." Burns frowns with concern. Now he cares if I attend dinner?

"I'll pass," I bite out.

"I'm starving," Jax says, glancing at me. "You sure you don't want to come?"

"Yeah, I have work to do."

Jax arches his eyebrow. "Are you sure it isn't because the women are pissed at you?"

"Buy them dessert, that will make them happy," Burns says with a shrug, hooking his thumbs in his suspender straps.

"I want to close Hattie's case before I head home." That will get Burns off my back and Jax isn't going to push.

"How's the case going? You have any leads?" Burns asks for the millionth time this week.

"Not yet, but my computer expert sent over some information earlier today," I share, shoving my hands into my pockets.

"Do you want us to bring you anything back?" Burns asks, still frowning, barely buying my excuse.

"No, I'll grab something on my way to the hotel."

"Suit yourself." Burns pats my shoulder before he and Jax turn to rejoin the group.

I take a step to turn when Sarah glances my way for the first time this week. The hurt in her eyes sucker punches me and I almost take a step toward her. I don't know what put the sadness in her eyes, but I'm ready to do whatever it takes to wipe the look away. Only, I'm not who she wants, so I hold her gaze.

McKnight puts a hand on her shoulder, which breaks the spell we are in. She looks up at him and he smiles down at her with a tenderness that he isn't capable of. I turn on my heels and leave. I don't want to leave; I want to tell Sarah she chose wrong. Warren isn't the knight in shining armor he wants the world to see him as, but it isn't my place, especially not with her expecting his child.

Driving back to the hotel in a hostile mood isn't the smartest idea. I'm already an aggressive driver, but I need to dive into work so I stop thinking about Sarah.

The information Cricket sent over will be a nice distraction. Most romance scams are run by individuals in other countries using fake names and photos, pretending to be looking for love. Once they find someone willing to correspond with them, they systematically break down their victim's guard before asking for money. They ask for small amounts at first, but then increase in size while still building their victim's confidence in them. The scammer usually cuts off communication once the money dries up, devasting their victims both emotionally and financially. If victims do step forward, there isn't much that can be done, but if this scammer is living in Peak Valley or River Bend, there is a greater chance of getting Hattie's money back and putting the scammer behind bars.

When I enter my hotel, I fire up my laptop and scan through the information again before calling Cricket.

"Are you sure this information is accurate?" I ask when she picks up.

"Hello to you, too," Cricket mutters through the phone. "You know my work is flawless."

"I know your work is flawless." I close my eyes briefly. "Walk me through it. If the person is close, I need to get the authorities involved, and I don't want them to have any doubt."

"The email address you provided is sending correspondences through a secure server, so I wasn't able to get much off it except that they used it with a few social media platforms. All dummy accounts with just enough information and pictures to look like a legit account. The pictures were taken from the real Hector Evan's account, who I suspect they chose at random. I used photo recognition software to tie the Hector Evan's photos to more than a dozen different social media accounts, all using different names but all living in Kansas, which is far enough away that it would be difficult to meet."

"Where does the real Hector Evan live?"

"Mexico. His profile was open to the public, so it was easy for someone to take the photos. He's pretty active as well, and his posts are in Spanish. I confirmed with Hector that he has not communicated with anyone in Kansas or Missouri. Nice guy. He's a grandpa and adores his grandbabies."

"So, Hattie's scammer is using Hector's photos and has half a dozen accounts, all with different names and locations in Kansas," I confirm, browsing through the different accounts Cricket had sent.

"Yep," Cricket chirps with a smile in her voice. "Pretty lazy if you ask me. Also makes him easier for us to connect other crimes to. We can nail his ass to the wall."

"Other crimes?"

"I compiled a list of individuals living in the retirement community who appear to have a relationship with one of the fake Hector's social media profiles. I found six individuals. I then peeked into their financial records—"

"I thought I said keep this legal," I interrupt, rubbing my forehead and trying to keep the annoyance out of my voice.

"I *know*. Just hear me out, boss. I thought if any of these six individuals had big cash withdrawals, you could speak with them. Save them from losing more money and—"

"And if they are still communicating with the scammer, I might be able to set a trap," I finish for her.

"Exactly! And you're welcome," Cricket says with a giggle. "You have probable cause to speak with them because you have evidence via the fake social media accounts."

"How many had big cash withdrawals?"

"Two." Cricket sighs. "Two too many, but hopefully, we can put a stop to the asshole."

"Shit," I breathe out, running a hand down my face.

"What?" Cricket asks with concern in her voice.

"I wanted to leave soon, but this case is going to take longer than I had expected."

"Sorry, boss," Cricket says sympathetically. "I have more bad news."

"Because my night can't get worse?" I mutter into the phone.

"You have to get the authorities involved. I know you have beef with the local sheriff. Or get your lawyer friend to help." I narrow my eyes. Cricket is incredibly smart but she's also nosy.

"How do you know about Sarah?"

"I don't know anything about Sarah, but I know you were with her the night you were shot," Cricket says with a laugh. "Did you really think I wouldn't read the case file?"

"I'm hanging up now," I bite out.

"Colson—"

"I'll talk to you later, Cricket." I sigh and hang up.

Fuck. If I want to bring justice to Hattie, then I'm going to have to grovel to McKnight.

Expect Forever

11
~Sarah~

Guilty.

It took the jury twenty-seven minutes to deliberate before finding Henry guilty. As a lawyer, it is always satisfying getting the conviction you want, but this conviction was personal. More for my sister Amber than for me. The feeling of relief and seeing the weight lift from her shoulders made it much more meaningful. I did everything I could to help her and knowing all that hard work paid off is more rewarding than I could ever put into words.

I hate myself a little for wishing I could have celebrated this victory with Eric, who was instrumental in the case. Without his quick thinking, we may have never known who was really behind the hit on my sister.

Even though he doesn't want to be part of mine or our baby's life, I couldn't help but watch him quietly slip out of the courtroom before anyone noticed. There is something wrong here. I know he told me we should part ways, but I have to be missing something. Or I just don't understand my feelings.

I should be mad, raging mad. Out for blood mad because how dare he abandon us, but all I feel is stunned. Is it the hormones or is this one of the many stages of grief? Amber and Dawn are ready to scratch Eric's eyes out. Logically, I know I should hate him, but I can't muster up a single shred of hate or loathing for him. When I try to think about why he would be so dismissive, I only get more confused. I never saw this coming. I never expected *him* of all people to disregard his responsibilities. Is it possible I never really knew him at all?

After the week listening to Henry's defense team try to paint him out to be an upstanding citizen, hearing a guilty verdict was such a relief. We all deserve a weekend without stress to celebrate and relax, but I just can't muster the energy to celebrate.

Instead, I came into the office for a few hours to get caught up. Five hours later, I force myself to stop and stand to pack up and head home. I don't want to become a workaholic as a form of escape. I need to pull on my big girl pants and accept my new life.

Standing from my desk, I start shoving case files into my bag while sidestepping the desk, only my heel snags on the carpet, bending awkwardly to the side. A sharp pain shoots through my ankle and up my calf, throwing my balance off. I try to grab for the desk but with my hands full, I drop them and fall hard, smacking my head on the shelf.

I take a moment to collect myself, filling my lungs and rub my stomach as a flutter of movement helps me relax before trying to hoist myself up. My ankle and head throb to the beat of my slightly elevated heart rate as tears flood my vision. Taking a seat in my chair, I tenderly touch my temple and wince when it stings. Blood coats the tips of my fingers.

Grabbing a tissue for my head, I carefully take off my heels, minding my throbbing ankle. My phone lays under the desk and out of reach while my orderly case files are scattered around the floor, along with other items that were in my bag.

"Sarah?" a familiar voice that haunts my thoughts calls my name. I jerk my head up as searing pain rips through the side of my head.

"How did you get in?" I choke out in surprise when Eric walks into my office. He stalks to me in a near sprint, dropping a thick folder on my desk before reaching for my face.

"What happened?" he growls as his eyes scan my face then down my body. His fingers probe at my face like a caress and relief floods my system, providing temporary relief to the pain my head and ankle are causing.

"I tripped on my heel," I whisper when he pulls the Kleenex from my head. Grabbing a few more, he applies pressure to my head, and I gasp a little at the sting. "How did you get in?"

"You left the door unlocked." He dabs at my head. "You should really keep it locked when you're here alone."

"I thought it was," I mutter, pushing his hands away and taking the Kleenex from him. The blood seemed to have stopped and the pain in my head fades. Looking down at my ankle, I notice it is already starting to swell, but there is no bruising. "Why are you here?"

"I was heading to your house when I saw your car in the parking lot," Eric says, taking a seat at my desk and crossing his arms over his chest. "We can talk about it later; you need to see a doctor."

"I'm fine. My head doesn't hurt that much now, and I don't think I broke anything." I lift my ankle up to inspect it better.

Eric presses his lips together and kneels close to my foot, his fingers featherlight on my swollen ankle, which sends a shiver up my spine. Eric stops and glances up at me. "Does that hurt?"

"No," I murmur, though I can feel a flush heating my cheeks.

"It doesn't look broken, probably a sprain. You won't be able to drive," Eric says and looks around at the small mess around the desk. "Do you need all of this?"

"Um . . . yes, but I can get it," I say, but Eric ignores me and begins to gather up the files.

"Do you want me to take you to the hospital or do you want to call McKnight?"

"McKnight?" I cock my head in surprise. "Why would I call him?"

Eric shoots a confused glance at me. "I think you should go to the hospital and get your head checked?"

"I don't need to get my head checked, I'm fine. Now tell me why you are here?"

"Sarah, we talk about this later. Is . . . is the baby okay?"

"I think so. The little bean is moving around like normal." I absently rub my stomach.

"I'll take you home if you don't want to call McKnight."

"I don't want to call McKnight, and I don't need you to take me home," I groan. Why does this man have to be so stubborn and confusing?

"Fine." Eric rolls his eyes, plopping my purse on my desk.

I lean forward to reach for my phone, but Eric stops me. "I'll get it." He kneels, keeping a hand on my knee. The warmth of his hand, the familiar feel of it, steals my breath and my whole body flushes. It's the closest Eric and I have been since February.

Our eyes connect as he hands me my phone, ensnaring me in a trance. There are so many things I want to say, so many questions I want answered, but I'm locked in his gaze.

"I should get you home," he murmurs, breaking the hold he has on me. All I can do is nod.

Before I attempt to stand, he snakes an arm under my legs and around my back, lifting me effortlessly. Both my arms wrap around his neck, clinging tight and holding on for dear life.

I don't want to swoon over him coming to my rescue, but I can't control my fluttering heart as he carries me in his arms. His musky scent conjures up memories of him holding me this close all those months ago.

"Can you grab your bag?" he asks, pulling me closer and his breath tickles my ear. I stare at him, confused by his words. "Are you sure you're okay?"

I shake my head. "I'm fine."

"Can you grab your purse?"

Mindlessly, I grab my purse and hold onto it while Eric navigates us out of the office to his truck.

"Can I get you to reach into my pocket for the keys?" He winks when I look at him in shock.

"I think I can stand." I squirm a little but he only holds me tighter.

"Stop moving," he hisses but gently lets me down on one foot, holding me to his side as he pulls his keys out and unlocks the truck. He doesn't warn me when he lifts up but pauses to scan his eyes over me before setting me down in the cab of his truck. He even fastens my seatbelt before holding his hand out. "I'll lock up. Is there anything you need in the office?"

"No." I shake my head, digging into my purse and finding my keys. "I can get it tomorrow when I get my car."

"Stay here." For a moment I don't think he wants to leave me alone, but then he shuts the truck door and walks back to the office.

I don't realize how tired I am until I have a few minutes alone in Eric's truck. Leaning my head back, I close my eyes, wanting nothing more than to let sleep take ahold of me and stop the thousand little thoughts that race around in my head.

I'm so lost in thought that I don't even pay attention to Eric when he climbs into his truck and takes off toward my townhouse. Maybe I should talk to him, ask him to explain. He's stuck with me in his truck with nowhere for him to go.

"Shit." My eyes pop open and I look over at him. Eric maneuvers his truck to the side of the road, and I glance behind us as flashing lights dance through the air and a siren blares.

"Were you speeding?"

"No," Eric snarls and I frown as he pulls his wallet out from his back pocket.

A deputy I've never met before but looks familiar strolls up to Eric's side of the truck and asks for Eric's license and registration. Briefly, he glances at me and nods before he collects Eric's information and returns to his vehicle.

Eric clenches his steering wheel and the tension in the truck thickens. I don't understand what's going on, but I don't ask, either. Minutes tick by and I start to fidget.

"Are you okay?" Eric asks, looking over at me, his eyes on my hands. "Does your head still hurt?"

"I'm fine. What's taking so long?"

"McKnight's minion is trying to find some bullshit reason to give me a ticket."

"McKnight's minion?" I turn to get a better look at the deputy, who is still sitting in his vehicle, his lights still flashing.

"Your boyfriend is a pain in my ass," Eric says through clenched teeth, and I jerk in surprise.

I frown at him. "McKnight's not my boyfriend." His hands clench tighter around the wheel before he side-eyes me. "Why do you think he's my boyfriend?"

"I assumed," he clips out, one hand releasing the steering wheel to rub his eyes.

"Why did you assume?" I demand, shifting to lean against the door, mindful not to jostle my ankle.

"Sarah—"

"Why did you assume?" I cut him off and he stops rubbing his eyes to turn them on me. The pain and anger chills me.

"You're having his baby. It made sense that you would be together," he says, pursing his lips and looking away.

"*His* baby?" I shirk. I must not have heard him correctly. "*Warren McKnight's* baby?"

"Everything okay?" the deputy asks at the window, holding out Eric's information.

"Everything is fine," I mumble, crossing my arms and sitting forward in my seat. I don't want to make a scene, so I bite my tongue.

McKnight's baby!

Where the heck did that come from. I think back to the day I told Eric about the pregnancy, recalling McKnight's early visit and Eric's quick departure.

"You have a border around your plates. It makes it difficult to see the information," the deputy says, handing back Eric's license and registration.

"You mean, the border that was put on by the *dealership*?" Eric asks with a bitter laugh. "I'll be sure to have that removed. Send my regards to McKnight."

"Have a nice day." The deputy smirks and walks away.

The drive to my townhouse is done in silence. Eric appears to be dumbfounded while I'm so angry, I fear I will regret whatever I unleash upon him.

When he pulls into my driveway, I grab my purse and open the door, ignoring Eric's protests. The cool concrete scratches against my barefoot. I'm about to see if I can put weight on my sore ankle when Eric takes ahold of my hips and lifts me up.

"Hey!" I screech as he slings me up into his arms. My arms automatically wrap tight around his neck as my purse swings up and smacks him in the face.

With a grunt, Eric narrows his eyes at me. "That was *not* intentional," I choke over a laugh, my anger defusing for a moment.

"Mm-hmm." Eric rolls his eyes. Using his hip to shut his truck door, he carries me to the front door. "Can you get your keys?"

Awkwardly, I unlock my door and turn the knob. The lights are off, but the fading sunlight still casts a glow over the living room.

Where my old apartment was elegant and sophisticated, my townhouse is inviting and cozy. Eric scans the room before carrying me to my plush white sofa covered in blush-colored pillows and blankets.

Eric gently sets me down, then silently gets to work propping my foot up on a pile of pillows that he places on my coffee table. Biting my lip, I watch him work. There is a tightness in his face and a stiffness to his movements. I wish I knew what he's thinking, but I don't want to be the one to initiate the conversation we so desperately need to have. I've been the one chasing after him, trying to talk to him, and he pushed me away. He misunderstood. He owes me more than just an apology, yet despite my anger and annoyance, I know I will forgive him. If I've learned anything as a lawyer, it is that we humans have a tendency to hurt the ones we love the most.

Once my foot is carefully elevated, Eric looks around, spots my kitchen, and walks away. I hear him rummage around in my freezer before returning with two bags of frozen peas. With gentle hands, he places a bag under my ankle before placing the other bag over it.

"Do you want some ibuprofen?" he asks as he takes a seat on the coffee table across from me.

"I'm fine," I say, biting my lip and pulling a blanket to cover me as the frozen peas numbs the ache in my swollen ankle.

We sit in awkward silence. His piercing stare could make a harden criminal confess their transgressions, yet somehow, I hold back from saying anything.

Eric takes a deep breath and lets it out in a groan as he runs a hand down his face. "I don't know what to say." He leans forward, placing his elbows on his knees. "You're not with McKnight?"

"No."

"And the baby?" Eric asks, concealing his emotions behind the stoic mask he wears.

"Is yours," I whisper as anticipation builds pressure in my chest. This is the moment of truth.

Expect Forever

12
~Eric~

Mine.

Sarah watches me with trepidation in her eyes and it guts me wide open. I move to join her on her couch, tucking her under my arm. She stiffens beneath me and nibbles her lip.

"I'm going to be a father?" I ask as excitement, fear, and relief overshadow the shame I have for thinking Sarah was with McKnight. I want to kiss the hell out of her, touch her belly, and whisk her away to Texas, but first, I owe her an apology.

"Yes," Sarah murmurs with a curt nod but doesn't relax as I pull her closer to my side.

I fucked up.

"I'm sorry," I whisper, pulling her lip from her teeth. "I should have never jumped to conclusions."

Her eyes swim with the tears she's trying to hold back. "You're right, you shouldn't have."

"Will you forgive me?" I pull her closer, not wanting to jar her ankle more, but I need to be closer to her. She's squished into my side but it's still not close enough.

Sarah releases a measured breath and looks away. "We're having a baby . . . and being upset with you will only make things more difficult."

"How far along are you?"

"Twenty weeks."

Twenty weeks?

"Five months. I think conception was in February, but they base it off my last period," she adds, and I close my eyes. I should have called her. I never called so she didn't, either. "I waited to tell you in person."

"Is it just one baby?"

"Excuse me?" Sarah pulls away from me and looks down at her belly, which is barely a bump. "Am I that big?"

"Is that not a question to ask?"

"No, it's pretty standard to have one child." Sarah shakes her head as she settles back into the sofa. "And you didn't answer my question."

"You're beautiful," I say seriously. Pregnancy has only enhanced her natural beauty. I thought that, even when I thought she was with McKnight.

"Eric?"

"Hmm?"

"Do you want to be involved?"

"Of course, I want to be involved," I growl, cradling her face. "There is no turning back now." *Shit!* I told her we had nothing to talk about when she tried to talk to me. I told her that we should part ways.

She nods and a look of relief relaxes the tension in her face. "We have a lot to figure out."

"We can talk about that later. Right now, I want to get some food in you and check your head and foot. Are you sure you don't need to see a doctor?"

"I would like to change into more comfortable clothes." She sits up and leans forward to pull the frozen peas from her ankle.

"Let me help." I take the frozen peas from her and stand. "Do you think you can put some weight on it?"

"Yeah, it's tender, but I think I can manage." She gently moves her foot back and forth a few times before letting me help her up. "I'll be limping around for a day or two, but I'll be fine."

"No more heels," I order and follow her in slow pursuit toward what I suspect is her bedroom.

"Are you going to wrap me in bubble wrap, too?" She laughs, glancing over her shoulder at me.

"If I have to." I wink at her. "Do you want me to order something?"

"Dawn left a frozen shepherd's pie I was going to throw in the oven. Can you handle that or is your cooking skills limited to ordering out?"

"She has jokes," I mutter, following her into a master bedroom. It's a warm, inviting room, even though the walls aren't decorated but the furniture is familiar. I remember it from when I stayed with her in Charleston. She's decorated the living room but not her room. Sarah stops and turns to face me.

"I don't need your help to change my clothes."

"This isn't dinner and a show?" I smirk at her suggestively and her smile fades. She doesn't trust me and that realization cuts deep.

"Go preheat the oven." She rolls her eyes while taking a step but wobbles on her feet. I'm at her side in an instant, wrapping my hands around her waist. I step in closer, pulling her into my chest, but she stops me with her hands.

Sarah looks at her hands on my chest and her chin lifts as she peers up at me through her lashes. Her cheeks flush with a blush and my dick grows hard.

Mine.

My head descends on its own, seeking out a connection to her. Sarah doesn't move, her breath warm against my skin. It has been months since I last tasted her and smelled her sweet lavender scent. I want nothing more than to bring us back together, but then she pushes me away.

"Sorry," I mumble, running a hand through my hair.

She turns away from me. "I'm going to change."

I watch her for a moment before leaving her room, shutting the door, and making my way into the kitchen. I find the shepherd's pie in the freezer and preheat the oven.

Fuck, I've made a mess of things. When she said she wasn't with McKnight, I thought my heart was going to punch through my chest. What kind of asshole makes stupid assumptions? *Me.* But that isn't like me. I follow the facts, but I didn't with Sarah and now, I may have ruined any chance of having a future with her.

Sarah emerges from her room wearing an oversized T-shirt and sweats, her hair piled on top of her head in a messy bun, and my semi-hard dick is at full mast.

"I think we should talk about the baby and come up with a plan," she says after she curls up on the sofa.

"Alright, but first I need to say a few things." I take the seat next to her and slide an arm around her. "Is this okay?" She gives a cautious nod, so I pull her closer. "And this?"

"Pushing it." She side-eyes me.

"And this?" I ask, pulling her into my chest, lightly pressing her head to my shoulder.

"Not appropriate," she groans, trying to pull away, but I hold on tight.

"Just let me say what I need to say holding you like this." I peer down at her. "Please."

"Fine, but only because you're warm." She relaxes in my arms and lets out a sigh.

"I promise to always keep you warm," I say into her hair. "I wish I could promise to never screw up again, but I think you know better than anyone that I tend to do everything wrong when it comes to you."

"Eric—"

"The worst thing I have ever done is let you go," I interrupt, rubbing a hand down her back. "I should have followed you to Charleston. I should have told you over Christmas that I wanted more, and most of all, I should have called you after I visited in February. I can't even begin to make up for it. I hope you know I'm sorry, and I hope you will let me make it up to you."

Sarah looks up at me, her eyes full of anguish. She's hurting and I did that to her, but I'd hope being honest with her will begin to repair the damage I had caused.

"Eric, I appreciate you telling me this, but I don't think it's a good idea for us to jump into anything. Everything has changed now . . .."

"Nothing's changed. You and I have always been drawn together. You and I have always found our way back to each other."

"And we always go our separate ways. The only difference now is that we're having a baby.

Yes, this ties us together, but that isn't a relationship, it's an obligation."

"Being with you won't be an obligation," I shoot back with a sinking feeling Sarah's already made up her mind about us.

"You say it isn't, but I will always wonder. Besides, it doesn't change the fact that my life and our baby's life will be here. You have a life in Texas, and I know Peak Valley will never be your home again."

"Is that why you moved here? Because you knew I wouldn't follow?" I regret the accusation the moment I say it. I don't stop Sarah when she sits up and pulls away from me.

"I moved here because I needed a support system. I felt isolated and alone in Charleston, and I wanted to bring our baby into this world surrounded by family and people who will love her . . . or him." Sarah's words pain me, but I can't argue with them. Here in Peak Valley, she has her parents, her sister Amber, and her best friend Dawn. Even my brothers are here. So many people ready to help her while I'll be in Texas, living out the empty life I've been living ever since I left Peak Valley.

"I see." I nod, watching her carefully.

"Will it be so bad that our baby grows up here?" Sarah shifts and lifts her legs to rest on the coffee table.

"No." *But I won't be here.*

"Good." Sarah smiles. "I want you to be our baby's life. I want her . . . or him to know you. We can come up with a plan that works for us both."

"Yeah." I nod, but I don't want to work out a plan that works out for us both. I want a plan where Sarah and I are together, raising our baby together.

Only that plan has to be executed here in Peak Valley.

Expect Forever

13
~Sarah~

The smell of bacon stirs me awake, pulling me from dreams filled with a faceless baby girl that brings a smile to my face—until I realize I'm not alone in my townhouse. With a groan, I flop onto my back and shove the covers off me, ignoring the need to use the restroom.

Eric's confessions last night played on repeat in my head, keeping me up most the night with more questions than answers. Just thinking about what he told me gives me butterflies and hope, but I can't let my longing to be with him overshadow the fact that he made assumptions about me and Warren McKnight. Not to mention the fact that he lives in Texas and never pursued me. Only now knowing I'm pregnant has he shown interest in a relationship. I'll never be first in Eric's life, and all the promises in the world won't erase my doubt.

I don't want to get out of bed, but I need to use the restroom. My stomach growls for the bacon that permeates the air.

I make a quick trip to the bathroom and make sure I don't look horrible before walking into the kitchen. "Morning," I yawn, taking a seat at the dinette table, spotting Eric's duffel bag by the front door.

He's leaving already?

"Morning." Eric glances at me over his shoulder, his blue eyes scanning my face before turning back to the stove. "Did you sleep well?"

"Yes," I lie over another yawn.

Eric pulls toast from my toaster and drops in onto a plate, buttering it before sliding an egg over easy and bacon onto the toast and closing it into a sandwich.

"Did you make me an egg and bacon sandwich?" I perk up, eyeing the plate he carries over and places in front of me.

"It's your favorite, right?" He looks at me with confusion before taking the seat across from me.

"Yes." I smile and take a huge bite. "Are you not eating?"

He smiles, pleased with his cooking. "I already ate."

"Are you heading back home?" I point at his bags, still holding my sandwich.

Eric looks over at his bags and leans back in his chair, putting his hands behind his head. "No, I'm staying here."

"Here?" I cough out, almost choking on my breakfast. He's staying here. Here in my house? What the heck is going on?

"Yep." Eric smiles like the Cheshire cat.

"No!" He can't stay here. Not when I'm trying to set boundaries—boundaries that will protect my heart.

"Why not?"

"Be-because!" I am not about to explain to him what I'm feeling.

"So, I'm working a case I need your advice on," Eric changes the subject. *Sneaky bastard.*

I narrow my eyes at him. "You're not staying here."

"I am. I need to make sure you didn't damage that pretty head of yours," Eric retorts, his stoic features softening into a smug smile.

"No."

"Should I call your sister or your mom?" Eric fishes for his phone in his pocket.

"Threats don't work on me. Call them," I push back, even though the last thing I want is being fussed over . . . and they will fuss. They will also concoct some insane scheme to keep Eric and me together.

"Dawn will want to bring over food and she's about to pop," Eric counters, still tapping on his phone.

"Don't. You. Dare." Using Dawn is going too far, and he knows it.

"If you won't let me take care of you, then you leave me no choice." Eric can't hold back that gorgeous smile of his. Did I mention he's a sneaky bastard?

"You're horrible." I glare at him, wiping my hands with a napkin. I then pick up my plate and take it over to the sink. "What is this case you are working on?"

"So, is that a yes, then?"

"Spill, Colson. I'm losing my patience," I warn, turning to lean against the sink.

Eric stands and grabs a folder off the counter, then hands it to me. "Burns asked me to look into a scam that was run on Hattie Smithson.

I think someone is targeting residents of the *Peak Valley Retirement Community*."

"What kind of scam?" I ask, flipping through pages clipped into the folder.

"Romance scam." He steps closer into my personal space and the urge to smell him is almost too tempting. When I did manage to drift off to sleep, it was his scent on my clothes that lulled me into a deep slumber.

"She was catfished?" I glance through various profiles, which all used different names but the same photo.

"Yes."

"Catfishing isn't illegal, Eric."

"I know," Eric says with a frown. "But many of these people sent the scammer money."

"Then you have a fraud case. Take it to the authorities so they can make an arrest. Did all these people come forward to you?"

"Not exactly. Burns set up a meeting with Hattie. I had Cricket, my computer forensic expert, look for others. We identified several potential victims through simple social media searches, but she narrowed it down by looking into their financials."

"I take it the financial searches weren't exactly ethical?" I look up at Eric, who purses his lips together. Yeah, he isn't the first private investigator I've worked with. They tend to blur the lines of the law.

"Depends on your definition of ethical." Eric smirks. "I only used the financial information to narrow down who to reach out to."

"And the others you contacted were also catfished?" I ask, scanning through the contacts he has listed in his file. Two elderly women, both widows. My heart squeezes. Sadly, this isn't the first, nor will it be the last time, I've seen the elderly preyed upon.

"Yes."

"What do you need advice on? It looks like you built a case for the authorities to take over and press charges." I snap the folder shut and hand it back to him.

"Is this enough evidence to get the authorities to press charges?"

"You need to identify the scammer. If you can prove fraud was used to get these ladies to hand over their money, then charges can be brought against them," I confirm.

"How likely will Hattie and the others get restitution?"

"It depends, but assuming restitution is part of the fraud charges brought against the person, then they should start receiving restitution payments after a conviction."

"So, it's possible?"

"It's possible, but I wouldn't make any promises."

"I haven't. Thanks." Eric reaches over and squeezes my hand.

"What are you going to do now?"

"Go talk to McKnight," Eric groans. "Do you need to go to the office?"

"No, I've got things I need to get done around here." I rub the back of my neck, thinking about the laundry I need to get done.

"Try to rest. I'll bring back dinner," Eric says as his arms rest on either side of me on the counter, effectively caging me in.

"You're not staying here." I try to sound firm but the tremble in my voice gives me away.

Eric searches my face, his emotionless mask unable to hide the pain in his eyes. The brief glimpse of vulnerability stops my heart. I don't stop him from tugging me closer. Tenderly, he kisses me while my stomach flutters with movement. It isn't lost on me that our baby is most active when Eric is around. Still . . ..

Eric deepens the kiss. It is no longer tender but full of passion and promises. I want to get lost in the passion and believe in the promises, but instead, I pull away. I feel the steady beat of his heart beneath my hands as he rests his forehead against mine. I don't know what to say; the more I push Eric away, the more he fights.

"I'm going to do everything in my power to win you back." He kisses the top of my head before releasing me.

Eric turns away, scoops up the folder he showed me earlier, and heads for the door. "I'll be back later. Try to get some rest," he says as he picks up his computer bag and leaves.

My hand covers my belly, feeling the fluttering beneath my hand. It's a moment I want to share with Eric. I want him to feel our baby move, but I how do I share these moments with him without losing what is left of my shredded heart?

14
~Eric~

"Janet! The jackwagon is here?" Burns hollers over his shoulder as he opens the door.

"Which boy is that?" Miss Janet hollers back from the kitchen.

"Eric," Jax answers, coming into the living room. "What's in the bag?"

"I need a favor," I grunt and drop the bag to the floor. "Can you hold onto this for me?"

"What's in it?" Jax asks but opens the bag before I can respond and pulls out one of Sarah's heels. I was hoping to keep the contents a secret.

Burns scratches his head. "Are you transitioning?"

"Transitioning?" Jax raises his brow at Burns while pulling more heels from the bag.

"You know . . . changing his pronouns," Burns says, pointing to the heels before he pats my shoulder. "I support you, Eric."

"I'm not transitioning," I bite out. I love Burns, but he can be exhausting. "I need you to hold onto Sarah's heels for me."

"What are you doing with Sarah's heels?" Miss Janet cuts in, carrying a cup of coffee and eyeing the shoes. "Wait, no, don't tell me. I don't want to know what's going on. Keep me out of it. I'm Team Sarah."

"Why do you have Sarah's heels?" Jax asks before putting the heels back inside the bag.

"I needed to be sure she won't wear them," I answer then suck in a breath before sharing my news. "She's pregnant."

"Sarah's pregnant," Burns repeats wide-eyed. "With a baby?"

"No, with a gremlin." Jax shoots him a sarcastic smile.

"Jackwagon," Burns mutters, smacking the back of Jax's head.

"She fell yesterday wearing these death traps." I point to the bag. "Don't get rid of them, just hold onto them until the baby is born."

"She's not going to be happy about this," Miss Janet calls from the kitchen. I know that, but I'd rather her be pissed at me than risk her falling again.

"I think a congratulations is in order," Jax says with huge smile and pulls me in for a rough hug. "Is that why she moved back to Peak Valley? Wait, does this mean *you're* moving back to Peak Valley?" The excitement in his eyes makes my gut twist. That will be everyone's first question for me once they all learn about the pregnancy, and I don't know how to answer it.

"I don't know," I admit, releasing my brother and rubbing the back of my head, hoping he and Burns won't press me on it.

"What do you mean, you don't know? You're moving here." Burns jabs a finger into my chest. Well, there goes any opportunity to skirt around the million-dollar question.

"It's complicated, Burns. I have a business in Texas, and Sarah isn't exactly *Team Eric* at the moment."

Burns narrows his eyes accusingly and takes a step forward. "What did you do?"

"I fucked up, but I don't have time to get into with you right now. I'm heading to Peak

Valley PD to speak with McKnight. I have some leads in Hattie's case."

"Is this little *fuck up* the reason all the women are mad at you?" Jax asks with that damn ornery smile of his.

"Something like that," I mutter. "Can you keep this between us please? I'm sure Clint and Luke will find out soon enough, but they should hear it from me."

"Sure, my lips are sealed." Jax rocks on his heels looking like he's holding onto a bit of juicy news, and he is. He's going to hold this over my head in the future, I just know it.

"I need to go. Be careful with those shoes . . . combined they're worth more than my truck."

Burns follows me out of the house. He wants to say something, and he isn't going to let go of whatever it is he has to say. "Spit it out, old man."

"I know you have your reasons for not wanting to coming back to Peak Valley, Eric, but I hope you don't let those reasons mess up a good thing." Burns isn't a serious man but when he has something to say, he always gets his point across. "All you boys have run away from Peak Valley thinking this place has brought you nothing but trouble. Don't make that same mistake again."

"Clint didn't run," I point out, shoving my hands into my pockets. I respect Burns; hell, he's been more of a father to me than my own was, but I'm not in the mood to hear what he has to say. Mostly because I know he's right.

"Clint hid away from the world and look what happened when he finally came out of his hole. This town doesn't have to be a bad memory . . .. It could be your future if you'd just stop being a stubborn jackwagon."

"Burns, I appreciate your opinion, really I do, but I've got work to do. Can we talk about this later?" I take a step down the porch steps, wanting to get away from this conversation and the heavy truth that's weighing on me.

"Whatever." Burns shoos me away with a disappointed frown. It stings seeing his frustration and knowing I'm the cause. Seems like I'm upsetting everyone these days, but what else is new?

Climbing into my truck, I shake my head at the decision I'm faced with. It's a no-brainer. I want to be in Sarah and our baby's life. I was ready to move to Charleston, but moving to Peak Valley makes things complicated.

Would the town embrace a private investigation company? I don't exactly have a good relationship with the Peak Valley PD and if they don't want me here, it will make running a business difficult. I have no doubt McKnight will do his best to be a thorn in my side.

No one is at the front desk when I walk into the quiet station, but I don't have to wait long. An officer who has pulled me over before walks up to the front desk and stares at me.

"I'm here to speak with Sheriff McKnight," I finally say when he shows no interested in speaking.

"Why do you need to see the sheriff?" he asks, looking bored.

"Business," I say laced with annoyance.

"I'll see if he will see you." The officer rolls his eyes and walks away.

Waiting is a skill of mine. You don't get into private investigation if you aren't able to sit still for long periods of time. A lot of what we do requires excessive amounts of waiting—waiting for information, waiting for a target to step out of line. McKnight probably thinks making me wait will piss me off, but it only solidifies my worries that he won't be willing to help Hattie and the other two women the scammer has stolen from.

"Colson," McKnight says with a knowing smile. The asshole thinks he knows why I'm here.

"McKnight." I stand and nod at him, not bothering with a handshake. It would only make him more suspicious. If I want to get through this conversation, I'm going to have to swallow my pride—something I never thought I would do when it comes to dealing with McKnight.

"You wanted to see me?"

"Do you have an office or somewhere private where we can talk?" I ask, unable to hold back the apprehension I have toward him.

He nods his head toward the door he came through. "Follow me."

I follow him through the small bullpen where his deputies work and receive a few suspicious glances as we make our way to an office in the back. McKnight holds open the door for me to walk through. It's a small office, but Peak Valley is a small town, and I wouldn't expect anything less. A lot of the pictures hanging on the wall are old, many praising McKnight senior.

"Is this your office or your father's?"

"There could only be one reason you would come here to see me, Colson," McKnight says, crossing his arms and not moving away from the office door, though he at least shut it behind him. I glance up and see all his deputies watching us through the giant window.

"And what could that reason be?" I question, mimicking him as I cross my arms with a teasing smile.

"You're about to leave town and you want to tell me to stay away from Sarah." He thumbs his chin.

"As usual, McKnight, you're wrong. I'm not here to warn you off Sarah, but since you brought it up, you should know she's taken."

"Taken? I guess we'll see about that." McKnight flashes his teeth.

"You'll stay away." I glare at him, dropping my arms and fisting my hands. "We're having a baby."

McKnight cocks his head, drops his arms, and searches my face. McKnight licks his lips and takes a step forward. I don't see the right hook he slams into my jaw and I stagger back a few steps.

"What the hell?" I yell, wiping at my mouth and seeing a smear of blood on my knuckles.

"Fuck," McKnight swears under his breath, shaking his hand out. "Your jaw is like a rock."

"Good!" I bellow, ignoring the pain in my jaw it causes. "I hope that hurt."

"Alright, Colson, you rubbed it in my face, but now I have work to do. I'm sure you can find your way out." McKnight walks over to his desk and takes a seat, opening and closing his fist a few times.

"Like I said, you were wrong. I didn't come to rub anything in your face. I came to talk to you about a case I picked up." I pull the file from my bag and drop it onto his desk and take a seat.

"A case? Someone needed your help?" McKnight gives me a skeptical glance but picks up the file and opens it.

"Burns asked me to look into it." I lean back in the chair and tenderly touch my jaw. He has a powerful right hook; I'll give him that.

"Hattie Smithson and Martha Goodright? Martha was my Sunday school teacher. She lives next to my mom." McKnight sits up, looking more interested in the case.

"Your mom is at the retirement community?"

"I moved her in a few weeks ago," McKnight answers to my surprise.

"Is your dad there, too?"

"No, they divorced when I was a kid . . .. You didn't know that?" McKnight looks up at me. "It was after your mom died."

"Why would I know that?"

"We were friends back then," McKnight grunts and looks back down at the file.

"We were?" I question, trying to remember that time in my life. Most of my early childhood memories have been long forgotten. I only remember the shit that happened after my mom died.

"Our mothers were best friends," McKnight notes, not looking up at me.

"Hmm."

"How far along is she?" McKnight shuts the file and leans back in his chair. "Sarah?"

I hesitate but tell him, "Twenty weeks."

"Twenty weeks?"

"Pregnancy is counted out in weeks," I say like I'm the leading authority on pregnancy. "Five months."

McKnight looks away. "I see."

"So, what do you think?" I nod toward the file. "Is this something you will look into?"

"Give me a week or two to look into this. What did Sarah say about it?" McKnight asks, steepling his fingers.

"She thinks fraud charges can be made if we can identify the person behind the scam, along with restitution."

McKnight nods then looks out his office window at his deputies. "Three victims total?"

"Three." I briefly close my eyes before adding, "They lost most, if not all of their life savings. I want to see justice for them. They are pretty embarrassed. If you take this case, you'll need to be gentle with them."

"I'll look into it *and* I'll be gentle. Are you heading back to Texas?"

"I want to see this to the end."

"I see," McKnight says, and I can't tell if that annoys him. "Looks like we are going to be partners."

Well, isn't that just great.

Expect Forever

15
~Sarah~

"I brought dinner," Eric calls from the living room. Startled, I drop the glass I'm loading into the dishwasher.

"How did you get in?" I ask as he drops two bags filled with Chinese food containers onto the kitchen counter.

"I have a key." He winks at me.

Sneaky bastard.

"I want my key back," I demand and hold my hand out. Give an inch and Eric will take a mile. He's making it so I can't turn him away.

Eric takes my hand and holds it, smiling down at me. "I'm serious." I try to pull my hand from his, but he doesn't let go. His other hand rests on my hip and pulls me into his chest.

I spent most of the day trying to figure out how I was going to handle Eric and his pushy, demanding, swoon-worthy ways, but all my plans disappear.

"How was your day?" he whispers down at me.

"G-good," I stutter, my breath catching in my throat as we both stare at each other. His nearness makes my whole body flush and my stomach flutters with movement. I lick my lips and stare at his mouth. He has such a great mouth, but the slight swelling catches my attention. "Wait. What happened to your face?"

"This?" Eric releases my hand and rubs his jaw. "It's nothing."

"Did you and McKnight get into a fight?" I step back, covering my mouth. "Please tell me you didn't get in a fight."

"Ehh." He shrugs, turning to pull the Chinese food containers from the bag. "Hungry?"

"Don't you dare shrug your shoulders at me." I smack his shoulder. "What happened?"

"We shared some words, he hit me, and then we went over the case," Eric shares as if it was no big deal before he hands me a container of sushi.

"He hit you?" I take the container, then hand it back. "Wait. I can't eat this."

He doesn't take the container and tilts his head. "Why?"

I push the container into his hands. "Because it's sushi."

He eyes me with a look of confusion as he pushes the container back into my hands. "Yes, that's why I got it. You love sushi."

"I can't eat raw fish while I'm pregnant." I put the container on the counter and take the chicken lo mien from him and sit down. "Why'd he hit you?"

"What else can you not eat?"

"Don't change the subject. Tell me what happened." I pull a knee up in my chair and dig into the food.

"He wasn't happy when I told him you weren't available." Eric brings over his beef and broccoli to the table. "Water?"

"In the fridge." I point to the fridge, though I feel a little unsettled. "Did you hit him back?"

He gets up and moves toward the fridge. "No." He chuckles. "I was in a police station surrounded by officers, all of which are his minions and just looking for a reason to arrest me . . . but I did hurt his hand."

I take a bite of my food while Eric hip-bumps the fridge door to close it. "Of course, you did. You're so damn hardheaded." I laugh when he glares playfully at me.

"He asked for a couple of weeks to investigate the case and talk to his district attorney, but Peak Valley doesn't have a computer forensic specialist. Small police departments like Peak Valley have to see if they can borrow one from another department." He places a bottle of water on the table.

"How long will that take?"

"I told McKnight I have a computer forensic specialist. While he is looking into the case, I will have my specialist take over communications with the scammer. We want them to keep the lines of communication open for as long as possible, which will give us time to gather as much evidence as we can." Eric sits down and takes a bite of his meal.

"That sounds simple enough."

"Not really. I need to set up an office to work out of. I'm having Cricket drive up tomorrow so she can help us."

"Do you have any ideas on where you will set up an office?"

"I was hoping you would let me work out of your law office." Eric raises an eyebrow at me.

"My office?"

"You have that large conference room severing as a storage room. I could set Cricket up in there." Eric wipes his mouth with a napkin and leans back, his meal half eaten. "Do you think Larry will be okay with that?"

"Um . . . I don't know."

"I'll talk to him tomorrow." Eric nods, watching me. "Is that going to be a problem? You're almost the owner, right?"

"Yes, I'm almost the owner, but I'm not sure it's a good idea," I tell him honestly. "You just found out I'm pregnant, you plan to stay here with me without my permission, and now you want to work out of my office? There are so many unknowns I think we need to figure out first."

"What is unknown?" Eric asks nonchalantly, looking at his food as if debating whether he should finish it off.

"You're plan, for starters," I huff, wishing he would share his thoughts instead of making me pull them from his thick skull.

"My plan?"

"Yes, your plan. Are you planning to move to Peak Valley? What level of involvement do you want to have in our baby's life?"

"I plan to be involved." Eric scratches his head. "I have a lot to figure out, sure, but I don't plan to leave, at least not until we figure it out."

"We?"

"Isn't this something we should figure out together?"

"I . . .. You want to figure it out with me?" I'm not surprised Eric wants to be involved, but I didn't expect him to want to work with me. He's always been the person who likes to tell you what the plan is.

"Are you seeing a doctor?"

"Excuse me?"

"A doctor, you know, to check on the baby. Aren't you supposed to see a doctor regularly? Clint is always going to the doctor with Dawn."

"Dawn is due next month, so she has to see a doctor weekly. I only have to go monthly until I get closer to my due date."

"When is your due date?" Eric rests his elbows on the table, watching me with genuine interest. His curiosity melts my heart and lightens the weight on my shoulders, but he's peppering me with questions to avoid talking about the big stuff—like this plan he wants us to work out together.

"November seventh." I feel a flutter and I rub my belly with a smile.

"Do you know if it's a boy or a girl?" He watches my hand on my belly.

Maybe the big stuff can wait a little bit longer.

"I'll find out at my next appointment, but I think I'm having a girl." I stand and walk to him. "Do you want to feel her?"

Eric turns in his chair and reaches up but hesitates before splaying his hand over my stomach. A flurry of movement dances underneath his hand and he looks at up me with a mixture of surprise and wonder. Love shines in those once cold blue eyes, stealing a piece of my heart as I brand this memory onto my soul.

"Does it hurt?" Eric asks, scooting closer. His other hand rests on my hip and he gently pulls me to stand between his legs.

"No." I laugh, laying a hand over Eric's. We stay like this for several minutes, feeling our baby move around, and it's hard not to want more of these moments with Eric.

*****

I stir awake, feeling a slight weight on my belly. With a yawn I open my eyes and stretch, finding Eric propped up against the headboard with one hand resting on my stomach and one of my baby books in his other hand.

"Why are you in my bed?" After we finished eating dinner last night, I didn't want to ruin the moment we were having, so I pulled out the sonogram photos from my past doctor visits. I showed him the nursery and we talked about themes I wanted if our baby was a girl. Then we watched some TV before I left him to sleep on the couch. He must have slipped in sometime in the middle of the night after my nightly bathroom break.

"This book says you can experience dizziness. Is that what made you fall?" Eric asks, once again ignoring my questions he doesn't want to answer.

"No, my heel snagged on the rug." I yawn again and grab my phone to check the time. My alarm won't go off for another fifteen minutes, so I snuggle in my blankets for extra sleep, but my bladder has other plans.

"Ugg." I throw the blankets off and get up.

"What's the matter," Eric asks, putting the book down, ready to help me.

"Nothing," I mumble and run-walk to the bathroom. I quickly relieve myself and wash my hands before climbing back into bed and snuggling under the covers.

"What time do you go into the office?" Eric shifts, curling himself around me, his hand once again finding my stomach. My boundaries are blurry; how can they not be when I let him—want him— stay close to me.

"I try to get in by eight," I say, automatically relaxing against Eric's chest. He sees this as an invitation and kisses my neck, sending tingles through my body and waking our baby. She flutters around beneath his hand.

"She doesn't move much while you sleep," he notes, his lips still resting against my bare skin.

"No, she doesn't," I whisper, hoping he can't tell I'm blushing. "She sleeps when I sleep. I think that's a good sign."

"A good sign?" Eric's breath tickles my skin, lighting up my core. I have to squeeze my thighs together to diminish some of the sensation. I don't think the easy attraction has anything to do with pregnancy hormones. I flat-out want Eric and that only makes resurrecting boundaries even harder.

"That she will sleep through the night," I whisper, pulling the blankets tighter around me. Apparently, Eric has other plans, and he snakes an arm beneath my neck and turns me to face him.

Even with the blankets separating us, we are too close. Absentmindedly, I lick my lips. Eric stares at my mouth, moving in closer, brushing his lips against mine. I can smell the mint of his toothpaste and I worry what my breath must smell like, but Eric doesn't seem to notice. His tongue runs against my bottom lip as his hand caresses up my back. I moan into his mouth, opening up for him as my hand traces his jaw, pulling him closer. We lose ourselves as we become reacquainted, until my alarm goes off, and I pull away, staring up at him breathless.

Eric gently slides a strand of my hair behind my ear and a slow smile spreads across his face that sets my heart racing. He moves over me and taps my phone alarm off, his smile turning mischievous. "You're much more agreeable in the morning."

"I'm taking a shower . . . *alone*." I push him away and untangle from the blankets. I don't look behind me as I climb out of bed, or when I close myself in my bathroom, though his soft chuckle heats my cheeks.

Eric isn't in my bed when I emerge from the bathroom, but the smell of coffee and the sound of the morning news playing on my living room TV tells me he isn't far.

I head for my closet and pick out a light pink dress suit that I pray I can still zip up. I'm getting by wearing my pantsuits and using a hair tie to expand the waistband, but I know I'm going to need maternity clothes soon. Maybe I can convince Amber to go with me on her day off.

With a little bit of tugging, I zip myself up—thankful I didn't have to ask Eric for help—and grab the matching suit jacket. Scanning over my shoe rack, I frown in confusion when I notice that most of my shoes are missing. Nothing else is out of place—all my clothes are there, my scarves and handbags sit on the shelves—but almost all my shoes are gone.

"Breakfast is ready," Eric yells across the house.

I close my eyes and let my head fall back in annoyance.

Sneaky bastard.

"Eric!" I yell and storm out of my closet. "Where the hell are my shoes?"

"You can have them back after our baby is born." To my surprise, Eric appears unphased by my obvious outrage and places a plate of pancakes on the kitchen dinette table. "Maybe."

"Maybe? Are you serious?" I tap my foot and slap my hands on my hips. This is the Eric I know so well. He doesn't ask permission, doesn't even ask for forgiveness; he just tells you how it will be.

"Dead serious." He peers down at me then nods toward my ankle. "It's still swollen."

"I'm pregnant, Eric. My ankles are always swollen," I exclaim and turn to walk out of the kitchen.

Eric grabs my upper arm and turns me back toward the table. "You need to eat breakfast. I read it's more important when you are pregnant," he says and steers me to sit in front of the plate of pancakes. "Eat."

"Not until you give me back my shoes!"

"You're not wearing heels, it isn't safe," Eric fires back and his mouth twitches upward.

I cross my arms over my chest. "You can't just waltz into my house and tell me what to do, Eric."

Eric studies me for several seconds before looking away. "You're right," he says, then points to the pancakes on the dinette table. "You need eat, then we can talk. Is that okay?"

"I can't eat all of this." I point at the stack. "I'm not your supersized brother Clint."

"No, but you are eating for two." He smiles, knowing I can't argue with that. "I read you can't have caffeine, either. What do you drink now?"

"Decaf coffee or tea," I grumble at the reminder. I don't want to give in, but I'm starving and the smell of pancakes is making my mouth water.

Eric gets to work making decaf coffee, making a point to check and make sure it is decaffeinated. He's already dressed for the day wearing a pair of nice jeans and a fitted dress shirt that shows off his sculpted muscles. I don't want to admire him; I want to be mad at him for stealing my shoes, but it's hard when he's pampering me at the same time.

"I thought we would drive into the office together," Eric says with a brief glance over his shoulder. "I can talk to Larry about the conference room."

"Do you really think it's wise we spend *all* our time together?" I pose the question before taking a mouthful of pancakes.

"Yes," Eric says in that stoic demeanor that only he can pull off. "Cricket thinks she'll get into town around three. What time do you get off work?"

"Usually around five," I say over a mouthful of pancakes and take the cup of coffee Eric brings over to me. "Where will Cricket be staying?"

"Clint and Dawn's old apartment." He sits and shifts several pancakes onto his plate.

I hand the syrup over to him. "I thought Jax was moving into the apartment?"

"He isn't too happy about having to stay with Burns and Miss Janet longer, but he knows it is for a good cause." Eric pours the syrup over his pancakes. "I'm rather good at these." He uses his fork to point at the pancakes. "I haven't had the time to do much cooking."

"That's a shame. I used to love the food you made," I admit, eyeing the last two pancakes.

"Used to?" He raises an eyebrow at me.

I lift a challenging brow. "Have you tasted Dawn's cooking?"

"Hmm," he says over a mouthful of pancakes. There is no arguing with that. Dawn is an amazing cook, and he knows it.

"I have no shoes to wear, I can't go into the office without shoes. Where are they?"

"I left *some* of your shoes."

"None I wish to wear." I stand to carry my plate to the sink. I devoured those pancakes. "I should mention that Larry will likely leave the decision to work out of the conference room to me."

"Are you holding the conference room hostage for those death traps that could have hurt you *and* our baby?"

"When you put it that way, you make me sound ridiculous," I cry out, turning to face him. "That's hardly fair."

"I think it is very fair." Eric pushes away from the dinette table with that damn smug smile of his softening his features. Why does he have to be so handsome? "I can't have you putting yourself or our baby in danger."

"You should have spoken to me about it before you went ahead and kidnapped every single pair of heels I own."

"Like I said, I left some. Do you need me to show you exactly where they are?" I glare at him and he moves to stand in front of me, barely leaving a handspan between us. "Besides, we both know you wouldn't have listened."

"And there lies the problem," I say with a pointed stare. I'm picking a fight. I know I am. I don't like picking a fight with Eric, but I need to establish boundaries, otherwise he will take control and cut me out of any decisions we should both be making.

He tilts his head in confusion. "Problem?"

"You make assumptions and act on those assumptions. There is no conversation with you. How could we possibly have a partnership if you're going to make decisions without talking to me?"

Eric's gaze is intense, and I want to squirm under his scrutiny. "Partnership." He says the word as if it gives him a bitter taste in his mouth. He wraps his hands around my face. "I don't want a partnership with you, Sarah. I want *more*."

"And I will never know for sure if you really do want more or if you are simply making a decision that you *think* is the best course of action," I whisper with tears burning in my eyes.

Turmoil rages in Eric's eyes as he searches my face. The silence between us is deafening, and my heart feels as if it's being squeezed.

"I made a promise to you, and I intend to keep it," he says. His words are enticing, but they don't wash my doubt away. I'm not sure if anything will.

Expect Forever

16
~Eric~

"What are you doing here, Traeger?" I growl when I see Traeger emerge from the rental car I had reserved for Cricket. She texted when she was pulling into the parking lot of Sarah's law firm, and I came to help her unload the equipment she brought up. I was not expecting to see Traeger, who was supposed to be in Texas acting as my delegate and making sure my business is running smoothly. His visit here could only me one thing—he wants decisions about his proposal. Decisions I have yet to make.

"Nice to see you, too." Traeger glares at me, popping opening the trunk.

"Sorry, Colson, but he insisted on coming," Cricket says with a shy smile, opening the back door. My dog Molly jumps out and runs to me.

"How's my brown-eyed girl?" I ask, crouching to pet Molly, who whimpers and rolls onto her back, demanding tummy rubs. Despite the sinking feeling I have at Traeger's presence, Molly and her subtle demand for attention calms my nerves. I scratch her belly for a bit before I stand and face my two employees.

Traeger narrows his eyes at me and crosses his arms in an intimidating stance.

"Can you two duke it out later? We've got work to do, and I'm *dying* to meet Sarah." Cricket rests her hands on her hips.

"Fine," Traeger mutters and leans into the trunk, pulling out a desktop tower. "Seriously, Cricket? Is *three* monitors really necessary?"

"Your fiancée is turning you into a whiny bitch," Cricket sneers at Traeger as she throws her computer bag over her shoulder and lifts a monitor out of the trunk. "Can you get the rest, Colson?"

I nod and tune out Traeger and Cricket's bickering while I gather up the rest of the trunk's contents. Molly sticks by my side like I trained her.

"Shit," I mutter under my breath. I forgot to mention Molly to Sarah. She never minded Molly being around, but it's just another thing I failed to talk to her about.

Cricket and Traeger continue to make snide remarks at each other as I lead them through the office to the conference room that will be a temporary workspace for Cricket and me while we help Peak Valley PD work the case.

Sarah was right about Larry leaving the decision up to her. For a moment I thought she was going to deny me the space, but she turned to Larry and asked if there was anything in the conference room he wanted to go through before giving me free reign to clean up and move the stored items into the actual storage closet.

Sarah's hasn't spoken much to me since her confession this morning. She's doing her best to avoid me and honestly, I don't blame her. I want to tell her that her doubt is pointless, but now I'm questioning all my actions. I have been making decisions without talking to her. I got myself into this mess because I didn't talk to her, but that doesn't mean everything I told her wasn't true. I want us to be together.

"What do you think, Colson?" Cricket asks, pulling my attention from my thoughts and bringing me back to the present.

"Excuse me?"

"The setup?" She frowns. "Were you listening to anything I just said?"

"No, I wasn't listening," I tell her honestly, shaking my head.

"Not surprised," Traeger mumbles barely loud enough for me to hear.

I ignore him and focus on Cricket. "Set up however you'd like."

"When do we get to meet Sarah?" she asks casually as she starts pulling cords from a tub.

"Never, she's busy." I roll my eyes, knowing I won't be able to keep Cricket and her nosy need to know everything away from Sarah.

"While she is setting up can we—"

"Taylor is my legal assistant; she has some paperwork we need you to fill out," Sarah says as she leads a client out of her office and past the conference room. "Thank you for coming, I'll be in touch."

"Sarah!" Cricket calls out as Sarah is about to pass us.

"Cricket," I hiss a warning, but she only shoots me a smug grin.

"Yes . . .?" Sarah enters the conference room looking at us with a hesitant smile and anxiety in her eyes. Anxiety I put there.

"Hi, I'm Cricket." Cricket raises her hand but her mouth drops to the floor when she notices Sarah's stomach. "You're *pregnant?*"

"Oh shit." Traeger's eyebrows raise to his hairline, scanning Sarah from head to toe. "Is this why you didn't move on the Charleston building? You plan to move here?"

A look of confusion and shock covers Sarah's face. "Charleston building?"

"Eric," Larry says, sliding past Sarah, oblivious of the chaos blowing up in my face. "Do you work adoptions by chance?"

"Adoptions?" Sarah and I both ask at the same time.

"No, not adoptions, really." Larry rubs the back of his neck sheepishly. "I have a lady on the phone who wants to try to locate her birth parents. I'm not taking any more clients, and this isn't something I'd typically work unless I need to have adoption papers pulled. Is this something you're familiar with? Can I give her your number?"

"Yes, yes you can." Traeger smiles at Larry and smoothly hands him a business card. "Hi, I'm

Traeger, Eric's *business partner*. We have worked several cases like this in the past."

"Wonderful." Larry takes the business card and smiles with relief. "This is turning out to be a wonderful arrangement." Turning to Sarah, he says, "Very smart bringing in a private investigator."

Before she or I can protest, Larry pats Sarah's shoulder and slips out of the conference room.

"What the hell just happened?" Sarah whispers, looking at Larry's retreating back.

"You two," I point at Traeger and Cricket, "get this place set up." Then I turn to Sarah. "Can we speak in your office?"

Sarah nods and backs out of the conference room. I follow her to her office, and Molly follows me into the office before I can stop her. "I hope Molly isn't going to be a problem . . .. I can take her to your place if you want."

"My place?" Sarah raises an eyebrow as she sits on the couch in her office. Molly beelines to Sarah, and she pets her absentmindedly. A good sign.

"Can Molly stay at your place?" I ask, wincing when Sarah narrows her eyes at me. "I'm sorry I didn't talk to you about it. Honestly, it slipped my mind."

She watches me for a moment then nods and leans back, covering her eyes with a hand while her other rests on her belly. Molly settles at her feet with a sigh. "Are you going to tell me what Traeger was talking about?"

Hesitantly, I take a seat next to Sarah. "Traeger approached me with a proposal after I met up with you in February. He wants to run his own investigation firm but starting up a new firm takes time. I was looking at opening a new location in Charleston, and he would take over our Dallas location."

Sarah looks over at me in disbelief. "Charleston?"

"I was looking at an office space not far from your office," I admit. Molly inches close to my leg and I scratch her ears. "Luckily, I found out you had moved to Peak Valley before I signed the lease."

"I see." She nods, absorbing the information.

Silence fills the office with an uncomfortable awkwardness until Sarah lets out a little snort. She snorts again, covering her mouth and trying to hold back a laugh. Her eyes are bright with tears, but not tears of sorrow, these are tears of laughter. I smile at her and she tilts her head back and laughs. It's contagious, and I can't help but laugh with her. I scoot over, taking her hand and placing my hand over her stomach.

"We-we're a . . . mess," she hiccups and wipes her eyes.

"At least we're together in this." I kiss her temple. "I'm sorry."

"For what?"

"For so many things," I admit, rubbing my nose gently against the side of her hair, taking in her shampoo's fruity scent. It's comforting after the day of confessions and secrets we've had, and I could use more comfort.

"Your business partner?"

I nod. "Traeger."

"He made it sound like you're planning to expand your business here in Peak Valley." She lays her head against my shoulder and I let out an audible sigh. Sarah hasn't willingly snuggled me on her own.

"Traeger is eager to be his own boss," I share, not sure how to navigate this turn in our conversation. "The fact that cases keep landing in my lap here in Peak Valley is promising, though."

Sarah turns to look at me. "But you never wanted to end up in Peak Valley."

"I know," I run a hand up her back, feeling her shiver beneath my fingertips, "but I want to be wherever you are."

"Eric, if we are going to do this together—raise our baby together—I need you to include me in the decision making. I know you can't flip a switch and make that change, but I'm willing to be patient if you are willing to working on talking with me before taking action and hoping for forgiveness," Sarah confesses.

"I can do that." I squeeze her, the heaviness I've felt on my shoulders easing up some. "I never meant to cut you out."

"I know, but if we want to this to work, we have to work together."

"I'll do anything to make this work," I tell her, tilting her chin up and softly touch my lips against hers.

*****

"You're so pretty," Cricket coos at Sarah when I bring her in to formally meet my team. "Is he blackmailing you?"

"Cricket," I growl a warning.

"No, he isn't blackmailing me, but he is holding me hostage." Sarah laughs when I glare at her.

"How far along are you?" Traeger asks in his interrogation voice.

Asshole.

"My team is more professional than this, and at the moment, it seems they're hellbent on embarrassing me," I groan, shoving my hands into my pockets. "I don't think they *want* their jobs anymore."

"Oh please." Cricket rolls her eyes with a mischievous smile. "You need me. Traeger, on the other hand, is completely useless."

"Eric may need you, but I don't," Traeger retorts with that stone-cold stare he's perfected over the years. It gets him results, but I don't like him using it on Cricket.

"Traeger, that look doesn't work on me." Cricket laughs with a wink. "I'm going to tell Zayne you used it on me."

"Don't you dare, bug." Traeger narrows his eyes at her but can't stop the smile from spreading across his face.

She smirks at him. "Call me bug one more time . . .."

"Who is Zayne?" Sarah asks, watching Traeger and Cricket with an amused look on her face.

"He's my surveillance specialist, but he mostly handles private security cases," I tell her.

"How many people work for you?" she asks curiously as she shifts on her feet.

"Here take a seat." I lead her to a chair that is tucked into the conference room table. "I have six specialists who work for me."

"Enough work talk," Cricket cuts in. "I want to hear more about the baby. How far along are you? Oh, what are you having? I bet it's a boy. Eric wouldn't survive having a girl."

"I'm five months along. I think I'm having a girl, but I'll find out for sure tomorrow." Sarah smiles, rubbing her stomach and glancing at me with an apologetic look in her eyes. She didn't tell me about the doctor's appointment.

"Poor beautiful baby girl." Cricket shakes her head. "Are you having a baby shower? I hope you do while I'm in town."

Baby shower?

"My sister is throwing me one this weekend. You should come." Another thing she didn't share with me. I can't say I'm annoyed; after all, I did push my way into her life without stopping to hear what she has to say.

"Yes, please!" Cricket claps excitedly. "I could use some girl time. I'm constantly surrounded by grumpy men."

"I can only imagine." Sarah chuckles and stands. "I should get going and let you get to work. It was nice meeting you both."

"I like *her*," Cricket whispers after Sarah exits the conference room. "Don't ruin it."

Yeah, I'm trying not to.

17
~Sarah~

Something is bothering Eric. "You're quiet tonight," I comment as I pull *Forensic Files* up on Netflix.

"I'm always quiet," he says, pulling my feet into his lap, his fingers quickly work to massage out the soreness.

"That feels amazing." I settle back and get more comfortable. "You're deflecting."

"I'm not deflecting . . . I'm thinking."

"About?"

"Your doctor's appointment tomorrow," he admits, pressing his lips together.

"What about it?" I try to sound casual. I meant to talk to him about it but thought our bigger issues needed to get resolved before bringing him to the appointments.

"I want to go," he says, still massaging my feet but watching me, trying to read my thoughts.

I nod. "Okay."

"You didn't tell me about it," he points out.

"Not intentionally." I look away. "I thought we had other things to figure out first."

"I see." He shakes his head and looks away from me. "Do you want me there?" he asks as a brief moment of vulnerability flashes in his eyes. As quick as it came, he tucks it behind that emotionless mask he likes to wear.

"Yes, I want you there," I tell him honestly, but I also want to know what his plans for the future are. He's made a lot of promises but hasn't been very forthcoming about how he intends to keep those promises.

Eric inhales deeply and visibly relaxes. He puts my feet down and takes my hand as he gently tugs me closer. I shift and move to sit beside him, but he has other ideas and pulls me on top of him, maneuvering us both so we are laid out on the couch, me on my side and him on his back. It isn't a long couch; I don't know how he could be comfortable, but the warmth he gives off is comforting. I lay my head on his chest and listen to his heartbeat as his pointer finger runs down my arm, tickling and tingling my skin.

"Do you really want to know if we are having a girl for sure?" he asks, his other hand playing with my hair. He's overwhelming me with his caresses.

"Yes, I'm ready to buy adorable outfits and decorate the nursery. I also want to settle on a name."

"Do you have a name in mind?" His featherlight touches become arousing and I bite my cheek so I don't squeeze my thighs against Eric's leg.

"No." I sound a little breathless.

Eric's finger traces my jaw, gently pushing my chin up so I'm staring into his blue eyes. I see hope reflected in his eyes—a hope for us, I'm sure. I don't know how it is possible to have the same hope yet doubt it, but right now in his arms, I want to ignore my doubts. I want to forget my worries and believe Eric is only here me, and not just because I'm having his baby.

As if reading my mind, he leans forward, his lips barely touching my own, asking for permission and I grant it to him. What started off as a slow caress turns into desperate need. Our tongues fight for dominance until we break apart, panting for air.

"I want you," Eric whispers with barely contained restraint.

"I want you," I admit with a coaxing smile.

"No, I mean all of you." Eric shakes his head, pinning me with those blue eyes and a silent plea for understanding.

I don't know what to say to him. I can't lie to Eric, nor can I pretend I have no doubts. Instead, I say nothing and kiss him with my own plea—a plea to forget our worries and just be in the moment.

There is a reluctance in the way Eric kisses me back. I know he wants more. I want to give him more, but I will give him everything and when he doesn't want everything anymore, it will break me.

Eric shifts, sitting us up and breaking the kiss. We stare at each other for a long second, him searching for what I'm scared to give. After a moment, he helps me up and leads me to my room.

My heart pounds with anticipation and desire. When we cross the threshold of the room, he turns around and pulls me into his chest before a finger runs down my face, tucking my hair behind my ear. He leans forward, kissing my neck gently. There is a promise in that kiss. A sweet promise that could obliterate my doubts, but instead of accepting the promise, I push it aside and pull off my shirt.

He stares at me as if I'm the most beautiful thing he's ever seen as his finger runs down my bare arm. I love when he looks at me like that. It excites me, washes away my doubt.

I reach behind and unfasten my bra. Eric sucks in a breath with a look of pure adoration that melts my heart. Tentatively, I reach for his shirt, tugging it up. He doesn't wait for my help but reaches behind his head and pulls the shirt up and over his head.

I don't even realize my hands are unbuttoning his pants until he brushes them away and pulls me into his chest, my baby bump pressing against his abdomen.

"Is this okay?" he asks, looking down but not pulling away.

"Yes." I nod, kissing him softly. The attraction I have for Eric has always been there, but it's been amplified by my pregnancy hormones and I'm growing impatient. I want him. Now. "Perfectly safe."

Eric pushes my pants and panties down with a trail of kisses stopping at my stomach. His hands frame my baby bump for a brief moment before he stands and guides me to the bed. I watch as he pushes his pants and boxers down.

I can't help but lick my lips at the sight of his hard cock. It has been too long since I felt him inside me. I want to beg him to come closer, but he remains in front of me.

"What's the matter?"

"I . . .." He shakes his head and comes to kneel on the bed over me. "It's nothing." Eric places open-mouthed kisses on my stomach, working his way to my chest. He covers my right nipple, and I can't bite back the gasp arching my back up.

I'm so sensitive to his touch. I'm breathless as he makes his way to my other breast, nipping at it. I comb my fingers through his hair as I wrap my legs around him, pulling him closer to feel him rub against my core.

"Please," I whimper when he tries to pull back.

He smiles at me with a teasing smile. "Do you want me?"

"Yes," I pant, digging my heels into his ass, pulling him closer. "I need to feel you."

"Do you want me to wear a condom?" His simple questions pulls me from the haze of arousal.

"What? No, why?" I lift up on my elbows. "I'm clean if that's what you are worried about."

"I'm not worried about that. I've grown used to having you bare," he admits.

"Have . . . have you been with someone else?" I ask, hating how pathetic I sound. I don't want to know, but I have to ask.

"Only you, Sarah. I've only ever wanted to be with you." He leans forward and kisses away my hesitancy.

I feel him nudge at my entrance, and I release a plea against his mouth. He is slow sliding into me, breaking our kiss as he watches me. I pull him forward, feeling him slide deeper. He feels amazing and I moan in its exquisite feel.

Eric strains against me but I need him to move. "Damn it, I need a moment," he growls when I try to move beneath him.

"Please," I beg, and he swears under his breath. I don't think he is going to move when he pulls back, pausing for only a second before sliding back in. The slow pace is going to be the death of me. My arousal is so intense, I might come undone before we even get started.

Eric's head rests against my forehead. "I don't want to hurt you or the baby," he confesses through clenched teeth.

"You won't hurt me or our baby," I breathe out with impatience. "Please move, *now*."

Eric hesitates for a moment before he moves, his thrusts slowly drawing more pleasure then quickly pushes me to the edge.

I bite his shoulder, not painfully but conveying my need, and Eric picks up his pace. His lips find mine and they're full of hunger and a longing that tightens my abdomen as I feel the beginnings of an orgasm ready to be unleashed. All rational thought leaves as I dangle over the edge.

"Let go," he commands, his movements becoming more urgent. I do as he says, letting myself fall and feeling the pleasure rush through me. All the emotions I held back wash away my doubt. Eric speeds up his thrusts, drawing out my orgasm before he roars out his own.

We both stay locked in an embrace, breathing heavily, utterly sedated with the most amazing coming together. Our sex has always been wonderful—we always knew how to pull pleasure from each other—but this time was different. This time there was a promise of a future I desperately want.

Eric has made good on his promise. He has me, all of me, but will he give me all of himself?

Expect Forever

18
~Eric~

Sarah shifts in my arms, her hair splayed out on the pillow. She looks peaceful in sleep. I can't take my eyes off her, afraid she will slip away. I watch her sleep, listen to her soft breathing, feel her steady heartbeat. She let me in with no sign of doubt lingering in her eyes, but I fear it will return. I don't know how to make it disappear for good, but I will do everything I can to prove to Sarah that I'm here for her and our baby.

Burns was right. I ran from Peak Valley, thinking it will never have what I want, but I didn't run toward the one thing I have ever wanted. Sarah.

My hand finds its way to Sarah's stomach—they always find their way to our baby. Sarah isn't the only one who thinks a baby girl grows within her. I thought it the first time I felt her move. I don't know the first thing about raising a baby. I may have helped raise Jax, was even his guardian for several years, but he was just a little boy when our mother died. Raising a baby is different. Raising a girl will be different. I haven't been able to tell Sarah, maybe even admit to myself, the fear I have toward being a father, especially to a little girl. There are so many evils in the world, and I want to protect my baby and Sarah from all of them.

"You're wake," Sarah murmurs, stretching and turning in my arms to face me. "Can't sleep?"

"You were snoring," I say, kissing her nose.

"I was not." She shoves me and I wrap my arms tightly around her.

"You were, just a little. It was cute." I chuckle, breathing in her sweet scent. I smell myself on her, and I want to coat my scent all over her, marking her as mine. Sarah mumbles something into my chest before biting hard. "Ow! What was that for?"

"It was a love bite." She giggles, snuggling in close. "And for the record, I don't snore."

"Sarah?"

"Yeah."

"The baby shower . . .. What exactly am I supposed to do?" I ask, sliding her hair away from her face.

"You don't do anything," she says with a soft giggle.

"Then what exactly occurs at a baby shower?"

"You play baby games, open presents for the baby, and eat snacks," Sarah sums up. "You don't have to go, but your brothers will be there."

"Dawn is about to pop. Is it a good idea for her to be throwing a baby shower?"

"She insisted." Sarah yawns. "She wanted to have the shower before she had her baby, but I wanted to wait until after I found out the sex of our baby."

"Tomorrow we'll find out? At the doctor's appointment?"

"Yes, then we can tell everyone a few days before the baby shower." Sarah frowns. "I feel bad not giving a lot of notice."

"It'll be fine. Dawn is about to pop, right?"

"Any day now." Sarah shifts to lay on her back. "I told her and Amber not to plan anything until after Henry's trial, but I didn't think it would push so close to Dawn's due date."

"Clint has been on edge. I think he's freaking out," I share, thinking about the phone conversation I had with Clint the other day. "He wants Dawn to take it easy, but she won't stop cooking and cleaning. I tried to tell him all the baby books say it's nesting and it's normal, but he wasn't really believing it."

Sarah's frown deepens. "He's nervous. I should cancel the shower."

"Don't worry. Amber is helping Luke, and I know everyone is excited about the shower." I try to reassure her, but her frown doesn't change. "Will you be like that? Do you plan to work until you have our baby?" I aim to change the subject and run a hand over her stomach, feeling a little movement.

"Probably. I don't like to sit still," Sarah says and yawns again.

"You should get some sleep." I tuck in closer to her, pulling the blankets around her.

"Mmm," she murmurs and drifts off to sleep. I watch her sleep for a little while before I fall asleep.

*****

"Why are you frowning?" Sarah asks as we wait for the doctor to call us in for her monthly checkup.

"Everyone is looking at me," I whisper, scanning the room full of new and pregnant mothers.

"They aren't looking at you." Sarah laughs. "Well, except for her." She points at the squirming baby in the woman's lap across from us. "She is definitely looking at you." Sarah pokes my shoulder and grins. "I think she likes you."

"What is taking so long?" I ask, looking around for a doctor or nurse.

"Relax," Sarah whispers, nudging me with her shoulder. "Why are you so nervous?"

"I'm not nervous," I lie, rubbing my hands against my pants.

"Sarah Baker?" a nurse calls from behind us. Sarah stands and I follow her through the door that leads to a small nurses' station where the nurse stops next to a scale.

Sarah puts her purse down and steps onto the scale. I watch as the digital display reads her weight. "Three pounds. Excellent, you must be keeping your food down now," the nurse says while writing in Sarah's chart.

"Thank goodness the morning sickness has passed," Sarah says, stepping off the scale. She grabs her purse, and we follow the nurse into a small room covered in posters of the inner workings of a woman's body.

"You know the drill." The nurse hands Sarah a cup then leaves the room. Sarah takes the cup and makes to leave the room.

I stand and Sarah turns to me. "Where are you goin?"

I give her a confused look. "Uh . . . I'm following you."

"No." She laughs. "Stay here. I have to pee in a cup, and I don't want an audience. Relax, I'll be back in a sec."

Sarah leaves and I take a seat, trying not to look around. I love the woman's body, but I don't want to see the insides. My knee bounces with nerves when my phone chimes and I fish it out of my pocket, finding a text alert.

Burns: *Have you found out yet?*
Me: *No. At the doctor's office now.*

Bubbles appears instantly but Sarah walks back into the room, so I pocket my phone and help her climb onto the exam table, ignoring her bickering about being able to do it herself. Not long after, the nurse enters and checks Sarah's pressure, noting that it went down. I make a mental note to ask Sarah about that later. After a few minutes, the nurse finishes recording Sarah's vitals and tells us that Dr. Rickers will be in soon.

"Your blood pressure was up?" I raise an eyebrow at her.

"I was dealing with a bit of stress," she admits, looking down at her hands.

"Ah, when I was going through my jerk phase." I nod and come to stand beside her, putting an arm around her. "I'm sorry."

She smiles and leans against me. "It's fine, Eric."

"It's not fine. I was a jerk, and I will make it up to you," I promise when Dr. Rickers knocks and enters the room with a smile. She's an older woman with kind eyes that sets my mind at ease some.

"Hello, you must be the daddy." She extends a hand. "Dr. Rickers."

"Eric." I shake her hand.

"How have you been feeling, Sarah?" Dr. Rickers gets to the point as she glances at Sarah's chart.

"Good, no more morning sickness," she answers, rubbing her stomach.

"Good," Dr. Rickers says. "Weight gain looks good. I'll look at your lab work when it gets in and call if anything looks abnormal."

"Okay."

"Any concerns?"

"None. I've felt good, tired but good," Sarah shares and I frown.

"She fell," I tell Dr. Rickers, who looks between Sarah and me.

"It was nothing. I hurt my ankle and barely hit my head," Sarah scoffs, rolling her eyes at me.

"Any nausea after the fall?" Dr. Rickers asks, standing and pulls her light out.

Sarah sighs and follows the light the doctor holds up. "No, no nausea."

The doctor pockets her light and returns to her chair to make a note in the chart. "Any headaches?"

"No, I'm fine. Eric is just overreacting."

"Okay, well everything looks good. Are you ready for the ultrasound?" Dr. Rickers asks Sarah.

"Yes, I'm ready to find out if I'm having a girl," she says, and my chest tightens with anticipation.

"Great, I'll send Ashley in to perform the ultrasound." She nods and leaves the room.

After a few minutes there is a soft knock before a young woman walks in with a bright smile.

"Hi, I'm Ashley," she greets, stepping over to the ultrasound machine. "Do you mind laying down?"

Sarah lays down and rolls up her shirt with Ashley's help. Ashley tucks a paper towel in Sarah's waistband before squirting some kind of gel on Sarah's stomach and presses a wand against it. A whooshing sound fills the room as a static-looking image appears on the monitor.

"That's our baby," Sarah whispers and grabs my hand. I'm seeing my baby for the first time and I don't have words. My heart wants to seize when the sound of a racing heartbeat drowns out the whooshing.

"A fast heartbeat," Ashley comments with a smile while pushing buttons on the ultrasound. "Do you guys want to know what you are having?"

"Yes," I answer before Sarah can, my eyes not leaving the monitor.

We watch as Ashley takes several pictures and measurements, clicking away at the ultrasound machine.

Ashley points at the monitor. "Okay, there she is."

"She?" Sarah and I both say. I look at Sarah, who has tears in her eyes. I kiss her sweet lips, wiping away her tears. I pull away with a big smile on my face.

"We're having a girl," Sarah whispers, then looks at Ashley, who is barely containing her laughter.

"We're you both hoping for a girl?" she asks, printing off a sonogram picture.

"I thought I was having a girl," Sarah says, watching the monitor that still displays our baby.

I run a finger along her jaw. "And you were right."

Ashley takes some more measurements and prints off more sonogram pictures while I try not to crouch in on Sarah, but I want to pull her in my arms, hold her, and feel our daughter move.

When Ashley finally leaves, telling us we can leave once we're ready, I wait until the door shuts before I pull Sarah into my arms and kiss the top of her head.

"Now we can start thinking about names," Sarah says into my chest.

"We can," I whisper into her hair, but first, I want to do something else. I pull back, frame her face with my hands, and kiss her. My kiss is full of promises. Promises to care for my two girls. Promises to protect them and love them with every breath that I take.

Expect Forever

19
~Sarah~

Saturday afternoon is looking to be a perfect day for the baby shower. The early summer weather is not too hot, so we all headed out to the back patio of Clint and Dawn's new house. Luke built them a beautiful house with five bedrooms and several bathrooms. Clint and Dawn aren't saying for sure, but I think they plan to have more children. The main floor is an open-concept layout with Dawn's dream kitchen and huge picture windows looking out to the patio.

Amber and Dawn decorated the dining room table with pink cupcakes, pink candies, and a giant diaper cake.

The men took one look at the diaper cake and headed out to the patio to grill burgers and steaks. The perfect weather drove the rest of us outside as well, lounging on the patio furniture. I'm not into the games and pleaded to skip them while we wait for the rest of the guests to arrive.

Cricket is one of the first to arrive and Eric introduces her before she takes a seat next to me.

"Please do not be offended by what I am about to say," Cricket whispers softly enough that Amber and Dawn can't hear. "How is your tiny friend carrying the Mountain's child?" She thumbs toward Clint, Dawn's husband. Clint is a beast of a man, and Dawn is a very petite woman but somehow, they make it work.

"It is a mystery we may never solve." I laugh and the doorbell goes off.

Dawn gets up and waddles into the house with Clint close on her heels. The poor man is worried she will go in labor while he isn't around and can't seem to leave her side, even when she isn't going far.

"I've never been to a baby shower but if I knew alcohol was involved, I would have made more of an effort to get invited to one," Cricket says, sipping on a flute of champagne.

"I'm pretty sure the alcohol was the only reason Dawn was able to get the Colson boys to attend." Amber chuckles, sipping from her flute.

"Mommy, can I have a cupcake?" My niece Emily runs up to Amber. "Luke said I have to ask you because you get mad at him when he spoils me."

"Luke said that?" Amber glares at Luke, who is doing his best not to watch the exchange. Cricket and I both barely hold in our laughter.

"Mm-hmm." Emily nods with a cheery smile.

Amber lifts her brow as she studies her daughter. "And have you already had a cupcake?"

"Mm-hmm. Uncle Eric gave me one, but I wasn't supposed to tell anyone," she shares, unaware that she isn't keeping any secrets.

Cricket giggles next to me. "Behold your future, Sarah."

"And Uncle Jax give you one, too?" Amber bites back a smile.

"No, but I haven't asked him for one yet," Emily says while tap dancing with impatience. "So, can I have a cupcake?"

"No, honey, the burgers will be done soon," Amber says in her mom voice. Emily pouts before drooping her shoulders and walks to Luke, who picks her up and coos at her.

Amber shakes her head with a smile. "He just can't say no to her." I look over at the exchange and Amber continues, "I will bet my next paycheck that in five seconds, he will put her down and take her hand, then they will look over here and I will pretend not to watch. Then, when they think the coast is clear, Luke and Emily will tiptoe over to the cupcakes, pretending that isn't what they are going for, and then Luke will slowly grab one. Then, Emily will look back over at me, nod at Luke, and he will pass her the cupcake on the sly."

Me and Cricket laugh as the entire scene plays out as Amber narrates their actions. Luke looks over at her and gives her a cheesy grin before joining the guys and Amber smiles softly.

"Hello, ladies," Miss Janet greets as she and Dawn walk through the patio doors. "Oh, we have a new person."

"Miss Janet, this is Cricket. She works for Eric and is helping with Hattie's case," I introduce.

"Oh, wonderful to meet you, and thank you for your help. Hattie is a dear friend of mine." Miss Janet comes over and hugs a bewildered Cricket before turning to hug me. "I'm so excited for you, congratulations. Baby girls are so precious."

"Thank you." I kiss her cheek. "Where is Burns?"

"The old fart is coming, he just needed some help with the gift he bought you and Eric. I want you to know that I had *nothing* to do with it."

"That's concerning." I frown.

"When it comes to Burns, you should always be concerned." Dawn laughs. "Does this present have anything to do with what he got Clint and me?"

Miss Janet frowns. "Yes."

"Oh no." I pinch the bridge of my nose. "Does he even know what a baby is?"

"What am I missing?" Cricket asks, finishing her champagne.

"Let's top you off first." Amber laughs, pulling the bottle of champagne out of an ice bucket, then pours herself and Cricket a heavy amount.

"Burns gave us one of those mini kid Jeeps for our son," Dawn shares, rubbing her stomach.

"Aren't those for toddlers?" Cricket asks and looks around—probably looking for a toddler.

"Yes, but apparently Burns doesn't know there is a difference between babies and toddlers."

I shake my head. "I can only hope ours comes in pink."

Miss Janet purses her lips. "Your assumptions are accurate."

"I've heard about Burns." Cricket snaps her fingers. "Eric's dad, right?"

"No, but he helped raise the Colson men," I tell her as Burns walks through the patio doors. His wrinkled face is full of excitement.

"Where are all the ladies at?" he hollers.

"They aren't your ladies," Luke hollers back.

"Jackwagon." Burns glares at Luke before shuffling toward us. "Don't get up, even though I'm old, don't get up. I'll come to you." Burns struggles to lean in and hugs Dawn. Eric mentioned Jax has had some concerns about Burns' health, and I make a mental note to talk to Miss Janet about it later.

"Now *you* can stand up, unless you're toasted," Burns says to Amber, who laughs but stands to hug him.

"Not toasted, but if Luke plans to let Emily consume an ungodly amount of sugar, I will be," Amber greets with a kiss to Burns cheek.

"The boy never learns," Burns mutters, shuffling in front of Cricket. "Who are you?"

"Hello," Cricket stands and hugs a bewildered Burns, "I'm Cricket. I work for Eric."

"Are you the lady working on Hattie's case?"

Cricket's smile widens. "Yep."

Burns eyes her curiously. "How'd the jackwagon get a good-looking girl like you to work for him?"

Cricket salutes Burns with her champagne flute. "Money."

"Smart woman." Burns points at her and smiles. "I like you." I haul myself up but Burns turns and fusses, "You should be sitting with your feet up."

"Ah, I'm not about to pop like Dawn." I pull him into a hug. "Speaking of feet, I want my shoes back."

"I have no idea what you are talking about." Burns shakes his head, though he takes a healthy step back. "Maybe Jax knows. I'll go find out right now."

"You do that." I wink at him.

"Shoes?" Dawn asks when Burns shuffles off to the grill.

"Eric stole all my heels, and I suspect he gave them to Burns." I glance at Miss Janet. "You wouldn't have any idea where they are, would you?"

"I told them to keep me out of their scheming. I'm Team Sarah." Miss Janet holds her hands up.

We watch as Burns points at Eric and they both look back toward me. I watch as Burns throws his hands up and Eric laughs, shaking his head. Jax walks past them, and Burns grabs his shirt collar, says something to him, and they both look in my direction but quickly look away. I have a good feeling that both Burns and Jax will be avoiding me at all costs today.

"So, Sarah, does Eric plan to move here?" Dawn asks the million-dollar question.

"I . . . I don't know." I scratch behind my ear and pick up my glass of lemonade. I was hoping to avoid this conversation, but I should have prepared for it.

"Him and Traeger finalized the deal on Friday." Cricket turns to look at me. "Did he not tell you?"

Amber leans forward and looks between Cricket and me. "Finalized what deal?"

"Oh shit," Cricket groans. "I thought you knew. After your doctor's appointment, Eric told Traeger that he was going to open the second location here in Peak Valley. That's why Traeger took off."

"So . . . Eric's back," Dawn says, watching me with concern. "Are you okay with that?"

"I'm fine," I tell her, though I am still a little stunned by the news. "I'm surprised but it's good."

"You don't look fine," Cricket says with a cringe. "Please don't be mad."

"I'm not mad," I tell her with a smile. "Surprised, but not mad."

Miss Janet pats my hand with a knowing smile. "Sounds like the jackwagon is getting his act together."

My smile grows wide. "Yeah, I think you're right."

*****

Eric and I are quiet on the drive back to my townhouse after the baby shower. My mind keeps going over what Cricket let slip. I have so many questions, but mostly, I want to know if this is really what Eric wants. I don't want Eric's move to Peak Valley be from a sense of obligation—I want him to want to move here. Want to be here with me, with our baby. Time over time he has attacked my doubt, saying and doing whatever he can to prove it, and it feels good knowing he's planning to move here. It feels really good, but will he be happy?

Eric must notice my conflicting thoughts and grabs my hand, linking his fingers with mine and giving them a gentle squeeze, which eases my mind a bit.

"Why don't you go lay down and I'll carry everything in?" Eric suggests when we pull into my driveway.

"I can help."

"I know you can, but I'll feel better if you go rest." He puts his truck into park and turns toward me.

"Fine." I sigh, knowing that pushing back will take more time than letting him carry everything in.

"Don't get out, I'll help you." Eric stops me from opening the door.

"Ugh, seriously? Are you going to turn into Clint?" I groan but wait for him to climb out of the truck and circle around to help me out.

"I think we need to start driving your car," Eric says as he helps me climb down from his truck.

"My car? Why?"

"My truck isn't safe for you to climb in, especially when you get bigger," he says, keeping his hands on my hips and pulling me in for a kiss.

"Sure," I say against his lips then smile. "As long as I get to drive."

"Don't push it," Eric growls. "I can be worse than Clint."

On that note, I give him a quick kiss and head into the house. Molly is waiting at the door, whimpering with excitement to see us. I spend a few minutes scratching her belly as Eric hauls in the first load of presents.

When Eric leaves for another load, I let Molly outside before heading into the nursery to put the presents away.

Everyone was generous with the gifts and it was hard not to get emotional in front of everyone. Burns did give us a pink Jeep for our baby girl. The man was adorable, ready to give her driving instructions when she's fresh out of the womb. I can't wait to see his face when he meets our baby and realizes it will be *years* before she can play with his gift.

Amber and Luke gave us a lot of the basics—burp cloths, swaddling blankets, a lot of diapers, and baby wipes.

Dawn and Clint gave us a diaper bag, one that made Eric cringe when he saw how frilly it looked. They filled it with more diapers and baby wipes and several onesies.

Miss Janet and my parents gave us so many adorable baby dresses and clothes that our daughter won't have to wear anything twice.

"Come sit down, you can put this away later," Eric says as he puts the last of the presents down in the middle of the nursery.

"I want to look at everything again." I pull out a soft baby blanket Miss Janet gave us.

"You'll cry, and I don't want to see you cry." Eric takes my hand and gently tugs for me to follow him out. "We can put it away tomorrow."

"Fine." I sigh, placing the blanket over the crib and running my hand over it before I follow Eric out of the nursery.

"Go sit down. I'm going to let Molly in," Eric says and walks through the kitchen to the back door.

I snuggle into the couch and turn the TV on, browsing through Netflix for something to watch and settle on a documentary Eric has been wanting to watch. Eric comes back shortly with Molly, who goes to her water dish.

"We can watch something else," he says, sitting next to me and pulling me into his side.

"I want to watch this." I hit play and stretch out on the couch, leaning against Eric's chest as he props his feet up on the coffee table.

Eric keeps running his fingers along my arm, my waist, and hip. He caresses my stomach, waiting to feel our baby move before running his finger over my hip and down my thigh. I've come to crave these little touches.

With each brush of his fingers, the more aroused I get. Eric is oblivious to what his fingers are doing to me. I want to tilt my head up and kiss him. I didn't use to be afraid to initiate anything with Eric, but since the pregnancy, I've held back.

Eric's finger traces up my side, setting my body on fire. When his finger traces featherlight against the underside of my breast, I gasp, capturing Eric's attention and he looks down at me. I forget my nerves and seek out his mouth.

Eric shifts, his arms come around my waist, and while never breaking our connection, he lifts me so I'm straddling his legs. A soft moan escapes me when I feel him harden against my core. We have too many clothes on. Eric reads my thoughts and his hands run up my back beneath my shirt, leaving a blazing trail, and I arch forward wanting to be closer. He momentarily breaks our kiss to pull my shirt off. He throws it somewhere before his mouth finds mine again and he grips my hips.

I grind against him and the friction heightens my arousal. Still too many layers of clothes separate us. I want to feel him inside me, deep inside me. Feel the passion we are so good at making.

Eric pulls away from me, his eyes black orbs full of desire, and I wonder if my eyes reflect my lust. "Not here," he says, and I'm confused until he wraps his arms around me and lifts us up. My pregnant belly makes it difficult for me to wrap my legs around his waist, so Eric places me on my feet and walks us to my room, stripping our clothes off with each step.

Eric lays me down on the bed and his hands roam over every inch of my naked body. I shudder uncontrollably with each touch, slow and exhilarating, coaxing a fire in my abdomen.

He looks down at me, ready to devour me, and it excites me knowing I put that look in his eyes. I run a hand down his chest, feeling the hard muscle twitch beneath my touch, and it's my turn to see him shudder.

His resolve snaps and he flips us, pulling me on top of him, guiding my waist over him. "Put me inside you," he growls against clenched teeth.

I wrap my hand around his hard cock and a sharp intake of breath from Eric washes me with a thrill of power I haven't felt since before we learned I was pregnant. I run my hand slowly up and down his silky shaft, a smile growing wide across my face.

Eric is quick and leans up, wrapping his hands around my face as his mouth crashes against mine, demanding I open up, but I don't let him have dominance over me. I push him back, shifting to guide his cock to my entrance. I slide him in slowly, relishing the feel of him stretching me until he's deep inside.

Impatient, Eric grabs my hips and moves me in a fast rhythm, but I resist, wanting to drive the pace. I pull his hands from my hips and place them over my breasts. I then roll my hips at a slower speed—one that will draw out the immense pleasure only Eric has ever been able to lure out of me.

Eric teases my nipples and I moan as it pulls me into an inferno of desire, picking up my pace until I'm grinding hard against him. He meets me thrust for thrust, giving back what I am giving him.

The feel of Eric's finger teasing my clit causes me to buck, setting off an explosion of stars before my eyes as I come hard and fast. Eric grips my hips and continues our rhythm until he groans and releases deep inside me.

I'm limp when I fall forward, but Eric holds me against his chest, both of us breathing hard with a sheen of sweat coating our bodies. Eric kisses my collarbone, and neither of say a thing. We don't need to; we both know how amazing that was.

20
~Eric~

A distant ringing pulls me from my sleep. It's a sound I've trained my body to wake and be alert to. Somewhere in the trail of clothes leading out of the bedroom are my pants, where my phone is, but I don't want to get up. Sarah is tucked into my side with one leg snaked around mine and her hand resting on my chest.

I listen as the ringing stops, only to pick up again. Sarah stirs, shifting and rolling onto her other side, allowing me to get out of the bed. Quietly, I tiptoe around our clothes, following the sound of the ringing until I see the faint glow in the darkness. It can't be too late in the evening if someone is calling.

The phone stops ringing by the time I get to it and doesn't ring again. Two missed calls from McKnight. I debate calling him back—it's a little after ten at night—but him calling means he's made a decision about the case. I know I won't be able to sleep until I know if he's going to help.

Looking around, I find my boxers and put them on before calling McKnight. Somewhere in the bro-code is a rule against calling another guy while in the nude.

"Did I wake you?" McKnight asks, picking up on the second ring.

"Yeah," I grunt, taking a seat on the couch and tapping my fingers with impatience. "It's fine. Have you made a decision?"

"I spoke with our district attorney. He approved moving the case forward, but he did emphasize that he won't be able to prosecute without evidence. I've got a pretty heavy caseload as it is, so if you only have circumstantial evidence, I'm not going to be able to work the case."

"Cricket knows what she's doing; she'll gather solid evidence that can be used to prosecute."

"Who's Cricket?"

"My computer expert I told you about," I say, running a hand down my face. "Come by my office tomorrow and I can walk you through what we have planned."

"I'll be out of town tomorrow, but I can swing by on Monday," McKnight says impatiently, piquing my interest. He isn't happy about going out of town? "Where is your office?"

"Where are you going?"

"I'm picking my sister up from the airport in Kansas City," McKnight says disgruntled.

"You have a sister?" Growing up, I don't remember a sister ever around McKnight. Several cousins, but never a sister.

"She's my half-sister." McKnight sighs. "My mom has early-onset Alzheimer's disease. It's why she is at the *Peak Valley Retirement Community*."

"Is she one of the scammer's victims?" I sit up, mentally checking the list of victims Cricket helped compile.

"No, I checked her accounts, but I can't watch her twenty-four seven, so my sister is going to stay with her until we wrap things up."

"I see." I breathe a little easy knowing that we didn't miss McKnight's mother. I might think McKnight is a douchebag, but that doesn't mean I want anything bad to happen to his family— except for his dad. His dad can drive off a cliff for all I care.

"Where are you and your computer expert working?"

"We're in the conference room at Sarah's office," I tell him with a smug smile. He's going to hate seeing Sarah and me together. Payback for trying to move in on her.

"I'll see you Monday," McKnight mumbles into the phone and then hangs up.

I click my phone off and head back into the bedroom. Sliding into the bed, Sarah turns to cuddle into my side. "Who was that?"

"McKnight," I tell her, getting comfortable. "He's coming by on Monday. The DA approved moving forward on the case."

She settles her head on my chest with a yawn. "That's good."

"Sarah?"

"Hmm."

"I need to tell you something," I say, sliding a hand through her hair.

"About opening a second location?" she asks, and I peer down at her. "Cricket let it slip."

"I should have known she wouldn't have been able to keep her trap shut long enough for me to talk to you about it," I grumble.

"No, don't be mad, it was an accident. She thought I knew." Sarah moves, resting her chin on my chest. "So, it's official? You're opening a private investigation office here in Peak Valley?"

"Is that going to be a problem?" I ask, needing her approval before I talk to her about the other plans I have.

"No." She shakes her head with a soft kiss to my chest.

"I'm going to need to find a permanent office."

"Yeah, I suppose you will need that," Sarah agrees, her finger tracing my collarbone. "Do you have a place in mind?"

"I do."

"Where are you thinking?"

I might as well rip the band aid off. I only hope she doesn't see this as me being pushy. "Your office."

"My office?" She frowns and sits up to see me better but it's hard to read her face in the darkness.

"You plan to remodel once Larry retires, right? That's what Luke told me."

"Yes," she confirms, not hiding her suspicion.

"The office is large for a one-person law firm. The expenses alone will eat a lot of your profits," I point out. "We could split the remodel expenses, building office space that would meet both our needs and lower both our operating expenses. Not to mention the additional benefits sharing an office building would give us both."

"And what are those benefits?" Sarah pulls the blankets up around her.

"If I pick up a case where the client needs a lawyer, I can send them directly to you. If you pick up a case that would need a PI's service, you have me there."

"I see," she says deep in thought.

I sit up in the bed, waiting for her to say something. "You don't like the idea?" I ask after several slow seconds tick by.

"No. I'm trying to phrase my words in a way that won't upset you."

Oh, this isn't good.

"Just spit it out, Sarah. I don't like my words covered in sugar." I roll my shoulders trying not to jump to conclusions. I've made that mistake one too many times.

"I don't want to make this decision because you and I are . . .. Well, I don't know what we are. I want to make this decision based on what is good for our business," she says more as a plea.

I breathe a sigh of relief before I reach for her and pull her back into my chest, tilting her chin so she can see me. "First, we are together. If I thought you wouldn't get upset, I would propose. Hell, I'd drive us to the courthouse and marry you if I didn't think you'd run away."

"Eric—"

I cover her mouth with my finger before I continue, "Second, I'm fine discussing the business partnership in a more professional setting. We should look at it without an emotional lens."

"Eric—"

"I love you, Sarah. I know I haven't said it, but you know I've never been good with words. When it comes to you and me, I haven't handled anything well, but that doesn't mean I don't care. I care. I care a lot, and I want us to be together."

Sarah moves my finger and whispers, "I don't want you to settle."

Frowning, I wrap a hand around her face, running my thumb along her cheek. "I'm not settling. I'm finally going after what I want. I should have done this a long time ago."

"Do you think you can be happy here? In Peak Valley?"

"Yes." I gently squeeze the back of her neck. "But I'll be happier if you'd marry me."

Sarah stiffens. "Oh."

"Think about it." I smile, touching my forehead against hers. "No pressure . . . well, maybe a little."

"Not helping," she groans.

"I'm happy, Sarah. I'm not going anywhere, I want to be here, and I will keep telling you that until you believe it," I promise and seal it with a kiss.

*****

Cricket is clicking away on her computer with her headphones on while I try to read my email, but that blasted noise is like fingers on a chalkboard. I'm used to working in my quiet office or out of my truck or hotel room when I'm on the road.

I'm about to head into Sarah's office when McKnight's ugly mug appears at the conference door.

"So, this is your office?" McKnight looks around before flashing a mega-watt smile at Cricket.

"Hi." Cricket waves. "I'm Cricket."

"Nice to meet you." He nods, dropping a couple of files onto the conference room table and tucking his hands into his pocket.

"Take a seat." I point to a chair. "You might as well get comfortable. We have a lot to cover with you."

"Before we start, I have some paperwork I need you both to fill out," McKnight says, taking a seat and opening a file.

"What kind of paperwork?" I sit up and peer down at the papers he slides to me.

"I'm bringing you both on as Peak Valley PD consultants. Hattie and Martha told me you were working this for free. Martha is an old family friend." McKnight slides papers at Cricket. "Bring you on as consultants will make it so my department can pay you for the work you're doing on this case."

I've been a consultant for other police departments in the past, even the FBI, but I didn't expect McKnight to want to work with me in any kind of official capacity.

When I first sought out his assistance, I didn't think he would take the case seriously. Now that he is, I'm stuck waiting for the other shoe to drop. The cynic in me shouldn't be suspicious, but I am.

"The pay isn't great, but it's better than nothing. You can fill them out later but get them back to me soon. Also, keep track of your hours." McKnight opens the other file and a notepad from his pocket. "So, what do you have for me?"

"Cricket, can you turn your display? We will walk you through what she's been up to," I instruct, leaning back in the chair.

"It will be my pleasure," Cricket says, turning her display. "I first monitored communication patterns between the two victims still communicating with the scammer. I focused on texting and email syntax. By reviewing the communication, I have reason to believe there is only one scammer as the syntax used is consistent in all communications across the victims."

"What do you mean by syntax?" McKnight asks, scribbling in his notepad.

"I study both the scammer and the victims texting and email patterns." Cricket opens two screenshots of text streams between two victims and the scammer. "Here is Martha's texts, and you'll see she writes long texts. The other victim, however, will send each of her sentences as a single text. Deviating from these text patterns could spook the scammer, so we want to make sure we mimic the victim's behavior. The scammer often uses the same compliments with both victims." Cricket points out a few of the compliments. "He also uses the same combination of emojis when he speaks with them."

"I see, so one scammer." McKnight scribbles in his notepad. "And you have taken over all communication with the scammer?"

"Yes. It's been pretty easy, and I don't think he's caught on. Of course, his texts are pretty benign. A lot of compliments and sweet remarks. He uses email to make requests, which is a problem."

"How is it a problem?"

"He's using an anonymous email address. I can't get any identifiable information from it. If it wasn't anonymous, we could have pulled his IP and traced it to his computer."

"Can you get anything from the phone he's using?"

"He's using a burner phone, which is similar to having anonymous number. We can see where it is pinging, though," I explain, pointing to Cricket. "Unfortunately, he doesn't like to place calls, so the ping data is limited."

"It sounds like you don't have much at all," McKnight exhales, leaning back with a grim look on his face.

"The pings are mostly coming from one cell tower," I cut in before he changes his mind about the case.

"Close to the *Peak Valley Retirement Community*," Cricket finishes, right as Sarah walks in.

"Oh sorry, I'll come back later." She starts to back out of the conference room.

"No, wait." I wave her in. "I would like your input. Can you sit in for a few minutes?"

"Sure." Sarah nods and takes a seat next to McKnight. "Hi, Warren."

"Sarah." He tips his head and smiles at her. I don't like him smiling at her, but I bite back my snide comment.

"We know we don't have enough data from the phone and email to lead to a suspect, but the pings being close to Peak Valley likely means the scammer lives in the area," Cricket steps in to explain.

"I can't knock on doors and ask people if they are scamming the elderly," McKnight says, crossing his arms. "I'm going to be honest . . .. I expected more."

"Well, if you would let me continue, I'll tell you about the other information I have." Cricket frowns at McKnight.

McKnight holds his hands up. "Fair enough. Please, go on."

"I built profiles for all the victims, not just the ones he's scammed, to see if I could see a pattern. What we know is they were all contacted by the scammer first. Either through the companion site or some other social media platform." Cricket opens several profiles she built and points to the similarities. "So, I thought, what if the scammer was targeting specific residents?"

"Targeting?" McKnight rubs his jaw, eyeing the profiles on the display, completely ignoring Cricket's glare for interrupting her again.

"If you look at the profiles of all the residents of the retirement community, many of them have social media accounts on the same sites that the scammer used. I'm trying to figure out why he reached out to those specific residents."

"He knows them," McKnight answers.

"That's what I think too, or he has access to their financial information," Cricket says, closing the profiles and opening another profile of the director of the *Peak Valley Retirement Community*.

"You think Dale Hurlburt is scamming his residents?" McKnight narrows his eyes at Cricket.

"I thought so at first, but when I looked into his financial records, and I didn't see any large deposits into any of his accounts."

Sarah tilts her head at Cricket. "How did you get access to his financial records?"

"I rather not say." Cricket smiles at Sarah. "I know that evidence can't be used now, but it does help us narrow the search."

"I can't go talk to anyone you identify through this method. I need probable cause," McKnight points out.

"I know, I know." Cricket sighs and opens another profile of Dale's older son Chris. "Just hear me out."

"Technically, you do have probable cause," Sarah chimes in. "You have a total of what, three victims who live at Peak Valley Retirement. That's enough for you to go question Mr. Hurlburt."

"She's right, but we also have a plan, but we want to be completely transparent with you about the plan," I tell McKnight, then look at Sarah. "And I would like to hear what you think of the plan."

Sarah and McKnight nod and turn their attention to Cricket. "While I was looking at Dale's accounts, I noticed he opened a checking account for his son Chris. When Chris turned eighteen, he didn't take his father off the account, so it appeared in Dale's financial records. I found large deposits into this account—deposits that match the amounts our victims gave the scammer."

"Chris Hurlburt is the scammer," McKnight says like it's a question.

"This evidence will help convict, but how you obtained the evidence would be thrown out. I could also argue it's circumstantial evidence," Sarah says while rubbing her stomach.

"That's why we want to set a trap that would point the finger at Chris," I reply.

McKnight narrows his eyes at me. "What kind of trap?"

"We think he is going to ask Martha for money soon. He's hinting at needing a surgery that he's afraid his insurance won't cover. When he does ask for the money, we want to tell him that a family member is putting a stop to the money order, but if he would video chat with her, proving he is who he says he is, she can send the money."

McKnight scratches his jaw. "That doesn't sound like much of a trap."

"Many scammers are put in this position," Cricket explains. "Often times, they pretend the video camera isn't working. We think he'll try that.

Once the video chat is initiated, we can get his IP address."

"If the IP address points to Hurlburt's house, you would have enough evidence to obtain a search warrant," Sarah confirms.

"I don't like it, but if it's all we have . . .." McKnight shrugs. "Set it up."

"It'll work. Chris has almost burned through all the money. He's going to want more. He's been living a cushy life for several months now, and he doesn't want to see that go away," I say confidently.

"I hope you're right." McKnight stands, gathering up his file and notepad.

"I know I'm right," I say. It has to work. This case has become more than just bringing justice to Hattie and the other elderly women impacted. This case's outcome will determine my business' fate in Peak Valley.

21
~Sarah~

It's Sunday morning, a week since Eric told me he loved me, and I haven't said it back. I don't know why I haven't. I love him, but every time I try to tell him, my nerves get the better of me and with each passing day, he seems more stressed.

We are eating breakfast and Eric looks lost in his thoughts. I debate whether I should pry and decide to broach a safer topic. "We should talk about baby names."

"We should." He nods in agreement.

"Do you have any names in mind?" I ask, hoping he does. I thought I liked a few, but after a couple of days, they lost their appeal.

"Not really." He shrugs, shoving the last of his breakfast into his mouth and stands to take his plate to the sink.

I frown. "You have nothing in mind?"

"My mother's name . . .." He turns and leans against the sink. "Elizabeth."

I tilt my head, repeating Elizabeth Colson over in head. I like the name, but I also don't have a reaction to it. "I've been looking at names for months now, expecting one to—"

"Fit." Eric nods in agreement.

"Yeah, like I would have some kind of reaction and know this is the name." I pick up my plate and carry it to the sink. Eric moves out of the way, resting a hand on my lower back while I wash my plate off. When I'm done, I turn to face him. His eyes follow his finger as it traces down my temple and pushes my hair behind my ear.

"Eric . . .." I'm about to say the words, but my phone interrupts me. Eric releases me and walks to the living room.

I pick up my phone off the dinette table, seeing Amber's name on the caller ID. "Hey, Amber," I answer, annoyed with myself for chickening out again.

"Dawn had her baby!" Amber cries happily over the phone, and my annoyance melts away, replaced with excitement.

"That's wonderful. I'm on my way." I turn and smile at Eric, who gives me a questioning look. "Dawn gave birth," I tell him, who smiles and heads for the bedroom.

"Okay, hon, see you soon," Amber says and hangs up.

"We have to hurry." I run into the bedroom.

"Why, the baby isn't going anywhere." Eric chuckles as he pulls on a pair of sneakers.

"Oh hush." I roll my eyes and head into the closet for my shoes.

Eric insists on driving my car to the hospital. He's been insisting we drive it all week. I don't argue, mostly because now that I'm six months pregnant, climbing into his truck was getting more difficult.

"I like Elizabeth as a middle name," Eric says when we pull into the hospital parking lot.

I look over at Eric's profile, surprised. "I like that." I really do like the idea of our baby sharing Eric's mother's name. I know he loved her very much and losing her hurt him.

"You do?" He briefly glances at me.

"Yes." I nod, relaxing into my seat. "We have a middle name, now we just have to come up with her actual name."

"What about her last name?" Eric puts the car into park.

"What about it?" I unfasten my seatbelt but don't get out of the car.

"Do you plan to give her my last name or yours?" Eric searches my face; his stress lines deepen and my face flushes with guilt.

"Yours." *Say the words.* "I . . .."

Eric nods with a big smile then opens his door before pausing to look over his shoulder. "Were you going to say something else?"

"No." I swallow and open my car door. Another opportunity lost.

Eric comes around the car, taking my hand and leading me into the hospital entrance. Peak Valley Hospital is a plain, four-story building. It's the same building my sister and I were born in. Eric and his brothers were also born here, and in a few months, it will be where our baby is born. So much history resides here, and I can't help but feel sentimental.

We ask the information desk for Dawn's room number, then take the elevator to the third floor. When we get off the elevator and head down the hallway to room 304, we are greeted by Burns and his Polaroid camera, snapping a picture of us.

"Before you go in," he stops us, flapping the picture. "Do you want in on the baby weight bet?"

"Bet?" Eric rubs his chin in thought. "How much are we talking?"

"Ten will get you in, but you have to make your guess before you see the baby."

"I'm out." I release Eric's hand to sidestep Burns.

"Your loss," Burns says. I turn and hold nine fingers up behind Burns back.

"I'm in." Eric pulls his wallet out as I slip into Dawn's room.

"Hey, momma," I whisper to a tired-looking Dawn. Clint is half-sitting on the bed with her watching Miss Janet like a hawk as she holds the little guy in a chair a few feet away. Amber is on the other side of Dawn's bed in her nurse scrubs, and Luke is sitting on a small couch.

"Sarah." Dawn smiles with a sigh. "Come meet Axle."

"Come take your turn." Miss Janet shifts Axle, and Clint jumps up quickly to help, carefully taking Axle from her. The love in his eyes as he stares down at his son brings tears to my eyes. I wonder if Eric will look at our baby like that.

"I hope he looks like me," Jax says when he, Eric, and Burns enter the room. "Everyone knows I'm the good-looking one."

Eric smacks Jax in the back of the head. "We only let you think that. You were a whiny child."

"Whatever," Jax grunts, rubbing the back of his head.

Miss Janet gets up from the chair, letting me sit before Clint places baby Axle in my arms. "Oh, he's heavy." I look up at Clint, who smiles. His puckered scar at the corner of his mouth has always made him look scary, but the pride and love in his eyes smooths away his sharp edges.

"Bets are in," Burns announces before snapping a Polaroid of me holding Axle. "How big is the big boy?"

"Ten pounds, two ounces," Clint shares and chuckles when we all stare at Dawn in shock. Clint is a large man—the largest man I've ever known—but Dawn is tiny.

"*How?*" Jax asks bewildered, sitting next to Luke, who smacks him in the back of the head. "Hey! What was that for."

"Is that big?" Burns asks, looking at Amber.

"He's a big boy." Amber nods, looking at Dawn. "I'm impressed."

"She was amazing," Clint says, peering down at Dawn with pure adoration. Dawn squeezes his arm with unconditional love. I look away from the happy couple, guilt settling in the pit of my stomach.

"So, who won the bet?" Jax asks a grumpy-looking Burns.

"Eric," Burns hisses. "I think he cheated."

"How did I cheat?"

"I don't know." Burns glares at him. "But I'll figure it out."

"What was your guess?" Luke asks Burns with an amused smile.

"I ain't telling," Burns mumbles.

"Come on, don't be like that." Luke chuckles but Burns ignores him. "Miss Janet, what was his guess?"

"Don't tell 'em, Janet," Burns growls.

"Was it something ridiculous, like twenty pounds?" Clint asks, grabbing a glass of water and handing it to Dawn.

"Who told?" Burns glares accusingly at us all.

"*Twenty* pounds? Really?" Dawn asks with an incredulous smirk. "Was I that big?"

"I don't think Burns has ever seen a baby before," I pipe in with a teasing wink at Burns.

"I have so seen a baby, just not one freshly baked."

"Freshly baked?" Amber scrunches her eyebrows at Burns.

"This freshly baked boy has a lot of hair." Eric smiles, running a hand gentle over Axle's head.

"That explains the heartburn," Dawn jokes.

"Heartburn means your baby will have a lot of hair?" Eric asks her seriously.

"It's just a saying," she says.

Eric turns to me, his eyes wide. "Do you have a lot of heartburn?"

"Some, but not much," I say, still staring at Axle in my arms. He does have a lot of hair. Black like his dad's.

In a few months, I'll be holding my baby girl. I wonder if she will have a thick head of hair like her cousin Axle. Will it also be black or brown like mine? Will she have Eric's blue eyes or my green? I'll be happy not matter what color hair and eyes she has.

"A little heartburn sounds like you're going to have a bald baby," Jax says with his hands linked behind his head. Luke slaps his stomach. "Stop that!"

"Stop being a jackwagon." Burns glares at Jax.

"Sorry, I'm sure Eric's baby will be beautiful . . . not if she looks like Eric," he says under his breath.

"She'll be beautiful, like Sarah," Eric says, running a hand down the back of my hair.

"Do you two have any names picked out?" Amber asks and I look at Eric.

"Are we keeping it a secret?" he asks me softly and I shake my head, looking back down at Axle still nestled in his blanket sound asleep.

"We don't have a name yet, but her middle name will be Elizabeth," Eric shares with everyone.

"Mom's name," Luke says it like it's a question and looks around at his other brothers.

"Is that going to be a problem?" Eric asks him.

"No," Luke smiles at us, "I think it's perfect."

"Elizabeth is good middle name for her," Miss Janet chimes in with a warm smile.

"You should name her Ericah," Burns suggests, coming to stand before us and snaps another Polaroid picture of Axle asleep in my arms. "Mashing names up is all the rage."

"Mashing couple's names is all the rage." Jax rolls his eyes.

"Ericah," Eric says, testing it out loud and our baby kicks me hard in the side as if answering to her name, and I gasp.

"I think she likes the name." I laugh, shifting into a more comfortable position as Ericah dances in my stomach.

"I like it," Eric says squeezing my shoulder.

"I named their baby!" Burns cries out, snapping another Polaroid of us.

"We'll never live this down," Eric groans, pushing the camera away. "And stop *taking* pictures."

Burns swats at Eric. "I'm capturing your memories."

"Why aren't you using your phone? It takes better pictures," Jax asks.

"I'm *old* school." Burns thumbs at himself.

"You're just old," Luke fires back.

"Jackwagons," Burns grumbles, shuffling to stand by Miss Janet, who pats his shoulder with a sympathetic smile. "So, is Ericah her name?"

"No promises, old man. We need to talk about it first."

"Well, talk about it," Burns urges. "You know I hate waiting."

"Too bad," Eric retorts.

"Do you want to hold him?" I ask Eric, who hesitates but nods. Clint comes to help, though I'm sure Eric and I could have handled the switch on our own. I bet Eric will hoover like Clint does.

When Eric takes Axle, he doesn't cradle him but lays him against his chest, his initial unease fades as he settles in the chair. "He is heavy," he murmurs, rubbing Axle's back.

"His appetite is just as big as Clint's." Dawn laughs. "I bet he will be twice his size in a week."

"The boy is going to be a beast," Luke comments, kicking his legs out and getting comfortable.

Eric's phone begins to ring in his pocket. He digs around for it while Clint watches him with annoyance and concern. Cricket's name splashes across the screen and Eric hesitates before answering it. Axle, not even bothered by the noise, slumbers against Eric's chest.

"What's up," he says into the phone. A soft murmur I can't hear chirps through his phone. Everyone is quiet while Eric listens intently.

Amber turns to Dawn and whispers something before she comes to me, giving me a hug and telling me she has to get back to work. She then kisses Luke goodbye, waves at everyone else, and leaves the room as Eric ends his call.

Eric tucks his phone into his pocket. "I have to get to the office."

"What's going on?" I ask as Clint comes over to take Axle.

"Cricket's set the trap," Eric says so only I can hear, then turns to everyone. "I have to get to work."

"Are you leaving, too?" Miss Janet asks me, and I look at Eric, who is watching and waiting for my answer.

I raise an eyebrow. "Yes, I want to help Eric with his case."

He nods. "I'd appreciate the help."

"Is that code for you two are going to do it in the office?" Jax asks, ducking when Luke tries to smack the back of his head.

"Wouldn't you like to know." I laugh as Burns walks up to Jax and smacks his shoulder.

"We need to go." Eric nudges me, and I quickly walk to Dawn.

"He's beautiful, congratulations." I hug Dawn, then hug Miss Janet, and wave at the boys as Eric tugs me out the door.

*****

"Hey boss, and *Sarah*," Cricket greets us in the office, and I make a mental note to find out how she was able to get into my locked office. "Congratulations on becoming an uncle."

"Thank you." Eric walks around the conference room table to stand behind her. His stress lines deepen, and I wonder how bad this case is getting to him. "Show me the recording."

"Recording?" I ask, coming around the table to see.

"I was able to get him to video chat with me," Cricket says, clicking away and bringing up a recording and pressing play.

"Did he put a fake photo over the camera?" Eric asks in disbelief. At first glance I was confused too, but after closer inspection, half an elderly man's face is visible. The mouth however, isn't. "That's new."

"I know, I almost spit my drink over the keyboard." Cricket laughs. "I hate admitting it, but I'm impressed."

As the video plays, it doesn't sound like Cricket but an elderly woman speaking through greetings and small pleasantries.

"Who is speaking?" I whisper not to drown out the sound.

Cricket pauses the video and points to a mic. "Me. My mic can change my voice. I switched between a grandma voice and my voice."

"He had to be watching the video. What did you use to display?"

"You can change your background with the video chat service we used, like a greenscreen. The background can be a video that plays on a loop. I created a video of Martha and her daughter sitting in front of a computer talking but then it cuts to a black screen that says, '*network is slow, video will start soon,*' and after a minute, it cuts back to Martha looking frozen in the screen before cutting back to the black screen. Basically, it looks like Martha is having internet issues, but the scammer can still see her. It worked like a charm," Cricket explains.

"That's genius," I whisper in awe.

"I know! I can be so brilliant, I surprise myself sometimes." Cricket giggles and clicks play on the recording.

We listen as Cricket pretends to be one of the victims. Her acting is flawless, and I'm blown away at her ability to scam the scammer. We continue to watch the video, which is over twelve minutes long, but the scammer sounds excited in the end, thanking her for helping to pay for his surgery. Cricket promises to wire him more money to a Western Union in Wichita in three days.

"You got his IP address?" Eric asks when we finish watching the video.

"Yes, and I already emailed it to McKnight. He's going to request the internet provider. Did you know there is only one internet provider here? Talk about convenient," Cricket sing-songs. "Anyway, he is going to put in a request for the home address. If it comes back to the Hurlburt's home address, he'll request a search warrant, but he wants you to go with him to question the Hurlburts."

"Good work, Cricket." Eric rubs her head, messing her hair up, and she turns and punches him. "Have you checked to see how many Western Unions there are in Wichita?"

Cricket frowns. "Too many to put surveillance on."

"Okay, can you make sure McKnight includes the Hurlburts' financial records as part of the search warrant?" Eric adds.

"Already did. Hopefully, we can wrap this case up in a week." Cricket clicks away on her computer.

"Are you ready to get back to Texas?" Eric pulls me into his side.

"Peak Valley is a charming place, but I miss Texas." Cricket powers down her computers. "When do you plan to move up here?"

"As soon as this case is over, and Sarah gives me some closet space," Eric answers and my head whips up. We never talked about where Eric will live when he moves. Yes, I assumed he planned to move in, but he never came out and said it.

"You want to move in with me?"

Cricket stands, shifting her eyes between us. "I thought you were already living together?"

"Yes, we live together," Eric answers, looking down at me as vulnerability flashes in his eyes. The guilt I've felt all week squeezes my heart.

"We are?" I raise an eyebrow.

"Yep, just waiting for you to give me some space," he says with a teasing smile.

"How much space are we talking about?"

"A foot, maybe two?"

"Sure, I could give that space up," I squeeze his waist, "as soon as you return my shoes."

Expect Forever

22
~Eric~

Sarah is looking through my business plan, carefully combing through it with a lawyer's eye while I patiently wait for her response.

"This is a solid plan," Sarah says, folding her hands on her desk. "Are you sure you want to split the remodel and rent office space with me?"

"That's the plan, but I would like some input on the remodel. I have some needs that this place doesn't have." I spread my arms wide and look around her dated office. "We also need to discuss hiring a receptionist."

"Larry's wife was the receptionist but retired, hoping he would follow her lead." Sarah nods. "Do you want to vet the receptionist?"

"This place is going to need security, too," I point out.

"I agree." Sarah nods. "How about you handle security, and I will hire a receptionist?"

"Do we have a deal?" I stand and walk around her desk.

"We have a deal," Sarah says, peering up at me. I lean down, wrap my hands around her face, and kiss her. Every kiss I place on her lips is a promise—and now I just need to convince her to marry me. Soon.

"Just received the search warrant. *Shit.* I didn't need to see that." McKnight turns his back on us. "Hurry, we need to head to the Hurlburts' house."

"You confirmed the address with the internet provider?" I ask, then kiss Sarah on the forehead before stepping away.

"Yes, and immediately requested a search warrant." McKnight turns. "Nice seeing you, Sarah." He waves and leaves.

"I'll see you later," I call over my shoulder and follow McKnight out to his sheriff's vehicle.

Leaving his lights off, McKnight pulls out of the parking lot. "I want you to let me lead the questioning. Is that going to be a problem?"

"No problem," I say with a smirk. "I want a conviction, McKnight. I'm not going to fuck that up just because I don't like you."

"Glad we are on the same page." McKnight smirks at me. "Let's go over what we know."

"We know Chris Hurlburt is scamming old ladies out of all their money," I respond, rubbing my forehead.

"I want to walk through the details."
McKnight circles his finger for me to spill.

"Dale Hurlburt, age forty-eight, married to Bethany Hurlburt, age forty-five, a stay-at-home wife. They have two kids, Lindsay, age nineteen and Chris, age twenty-one."

"What do we know about Dale?" McKnight fires off.

"He's been the director of *Peak Valley Retirement Community* for fifteen years. Lives at the Retirement Community as part of the gig. He works out of a home office. Doesn't have any priors, doesn't even have a speeding ticket."

"And Chris?"

"Wasn't a stellar student, barely made it into college. Attended K-State, but after a minor possession charge, he failed out and returned home. Works for his father as part of the lawn crew," I finish as McKnight stops at a light. "What else do you want to know?"

"Just wanted to make sure you knew the case forward and backward," McKnight says as the light turns green, and he takes off.

"You were testing me? I brought this case to you," I scoff. "You really don't like to play nice with others, do you?"

"I always play nice." McKnight chuckles. "You know, I've never had a problem with you. This feud we have . . . you started it." He points at me.

"That good old boy routine may fool everyone, but it doesn't fool me." I laugh. "You're just like your father."

"You're an asshole, Colson," McKnight says, gripping tight on the steering wheel. "I don't know why my father had it out for you and your brothers. I didn't like it."

"And pulling me over for bullshit reasons?"

"Well, that was just funny. You get so pissed off." McKnight laughs. "You never got a ticket."

"What about Luke?"

"What about Luke?" McKnight asks, pulling into the Hurlburts' driveway.

"Why did you detain him? You knew he had nothing to do with the shooting at Amber's."

"I followed protocol," McKnight defends. "I can't let biases impact my judgment. You should know that better than anyone."

"C'mon, let's go question Dale Hurlburt." I open the car door, ready to end this conversation. I want to believe McKnight has an answer for everything, but my gut is telling me I may have been wrong about him. And my gut's never wrong.

Bethany Hurlburt answers the door after we ring the doorbell. Once she sees McKnight, her welcome smile fades, quickly turning to a bone-chilling fear. It isn't uncommon for someone to be confused when the authorities are at their door, even reluctance is normal, but fear means she knows why we're here.

"Hello, Mrs. Hurlburt. Is your husband home?" McKnight flashes her a charming smile.

"You . . . you want to see Dale?" She swallows, glancing over her shoulder. "He's working."

"We just have a few questions for him, Mrs. Hurlburt." I try to reassure her with my warm smile.

"I'm sorry, who are you?" Bethany asks, rubbing her arms.

"Eric Colson, I'm a private investigator."

"I didn't know Peak Valley had a private investigator." She nods and shifts on her feet, though she does not let us come inside the home.

"He works out of Larry Rutledge's law firm," McKnight shares. "Can we come inside and speak with your husband?"

"Oh, I'm not sure that is a good idea." Mrs. Hurlburt shakes her head and desperation fills her eyes. "He's really busy. Maybe you should come back another time."

"Mrs. Hurlburt," McKnight takes a step closer to the door, "is everything okay?"

"Yes, of course everything is okay," Mrs. Hurlburt says quickly, dropping her arms. "Why wouldn't it be okay?"

"You seem a little nervous," McKnight says. "If you need help, you can tell me."

"*No*, no." She shakes her head and then opens the door wide, letting us in. "I don't need help." She fidgets for a moment, glancing up at the stairs. "Follow me, I'll take you to his office."

Mrs. Hurlburt glances up the stairs twice but leads us past them to closed double doors off the main hallway. "Dale?" She knocks softly before opening his office doors. "Sherriff McKnight is here to speak with you, and . . . I'm sorry, I forgot your name."

"Eric Colson." I walk into the office with McKnight.

"What is this about?" Mr. Hurlburt stands from his desk, pulling his glasses off.

"We would like to talk to you about a case we are working," McKnight gets to the point and takes a seat at a chair that sits in front of Mr. Hurlburt's desk. I follow and take a seat in the chair next to McKnight.

"A case?" Mr. Hurlburt sits down with a frown.

Glancing over my shoulder, I see Mrs. Hurlburt stand by the office doors looking toward the stairs. I don't like the way she's fidgeting. She knows something. Mothers always know what is going on in their kid's lives. My gut tells me we're questioning the wrong person, but I let McKnight take the lead.

"We have reason to believe someone is stealing from the residents of your retirement home," McKnight shares.

Mr. Hurlburt's eyebrows slump in confusion. "My residents?"

"Yes, we have confirmation." McKnight pulls a photo. "Do you know this person?"

Mr. Hurlburt puts his glasses back on and peers down at the photo for several seconds. "No, no, I can't say I do. Is this the person stealing from my residents?"

"No, we don't think he is the person responsible, but we do believe his identity is being used to trick your residents out of their life savings." McKnight pulls the photo back. "We also believe that person lives here."

"What do you mean . . . lives here?" Mrs. Hurlburt asks, stepping into the office.

"Do you think *I'm* behind this?" Mr. Hurlburt asks, outraged.

"We're not saying that," McKnight says, scooting to the edge of his seat. "But if you would allow us to search your computers—"

"No," Mrs. Hurlburt cries out, visibly shaking.

"Bethany?" Mr. Hurlburt stands, eyeing her with concern.

"You can't," she repeats glancing behind her again.

"Where is your son?" I stand and slowly approach Mrs. Hurlburt, who shakes her head.

"I . . . I don't know." She continues to shake her head with tears brimming her eyes.

"Bethany." Dale puts his hands on his hips. "He's upstairs. In his room."

"No, no, he's not." Mrs. Hurlburt steps away from me as McKnight leaves the office.

"Mr. Hurlburt, we have a search warrant." I look at a devastated man. "We need all the computers in your home."

Mr. Hurlburt glances at his wife.

"Dale, don't let them," Mrs. Hurlburt pleads as I move past her.

McKnight is halfway up the stairs when we hear tires peel out. I go to the door and look out to see a red mustang speed down the street, too far away to get the plates.

"Please, Chris a good boy." Mrs. Hurlburt comes out of the study with Mr. Hurlburt. "He's a *good* boy."

"Mrs. Hurlburt, do you know what your son has been up to?" I ask as McKnight appears at the top of the stairs.

"We've been asking him how he's been getting all this extra cash." Mr. Hurlburt puts an arm around his wife. "We thought it was drugs, but he told us he has been building websites on the side."

"Chris didn't do this," Mrs. Hurlburt pleads with us. "He wouldn't steal from anyone."

"Was that his red mustang?" I ask, McKnight joining us by the door.

"Yes," Mr. Hurlburt says.

"I'm call a deputy to come over and collect your computers." McKnight pulls out the search warrant and hands it to Mr. Hurlburt. "Do you know where your son would go?"

"He has a friend who lives in River Bend, Mitch . . .." Mr. Hurlburt looks at his wife. "What is Mitch's last name?"

"Easton, I think," Mrs. Hurlburt whimpers next to her husband.

"Thank you." McKnight nods and radios the information to dispatch. "Take a seat please."

"Did you find Chris' computer?" I ask quietly.

"No, he must have taken it with him," McKnight shares with me. "I called all available deputies on patrol to be on the lookout. We'll find him, but we can't leave until I get someone up here to confiscate the computers. I don't trust the wife not to try and *help* her son."

I glance at Mrs. Hurlburt. "Yeah, I agree."

23
~Sarah~

These IT service provider quotes might as well be written in gibberish. I thought getting a quote for setting up some computers, software, and a website would be easy, but there are line items that make no sense to me.

What the heck is a domain?

"Hey, Cricket?" I knock on the conference room door. "Do you mind looking at these for me?"

"What am I looking at?" She stops her clicking and I slide the quotes across the table to her.

"IT service provider quotes." I take a seat across from her and sigh. My ankles are swelling more as the summer temperatures rise. I'll never admit this to Eric, but with my swollen ankles, there is no way I could wear the heels he stole.

"Oh goody. I get to tell you who's a moron and who isn't." Cricket picks up the quotes. "You know, you could have Eric pay me to set everything up."

"Really? You would want to do that?" I rub the back of my neck. I'd much rather have Cricket set everything up. I trust her more than a nameless technician.

"I love this kind of thing. Besides, I'm going to have to do some tech setup for Eric when this place gets remodeled. Might as well pay me to do it all."

"Well, in that case, I'll take you up on the offer." I laugh, about to stand, when a man in a hoodie storms into the conference room, pointing a gun at Cricket.

"Is that where the evidence is?" he demands, waving the gun at Cricket's computers.

Cricket holds her hands up and I cover my stomach, pushing my chair away from the man. "I don't know what you're talking about," Cricket says calmly, her face pale.

"Don't lie to me!" He steps closer to her then turns the gun on me. His face is visible, and I instantly recognize him. I let out a cry and try to push myself out of the line of fire. "Don't move!"

"O-okay, I won't move." I hold my hands up. My heart is racing, panic making it hard to breathe. Chris Hurlburt glares at me, his face tight with anger and fear. "Please, don't point that gun at me."

"I want the evidence." He waves the gun up and down at me, then points it back at Cricket. "I know it's here."

"Please, I'm a lawyer. I can help you with whatever trouble you're in, but first, you have to put the gun down." I can't keep the tremble out of my voice. My heart continues to pound in my chest like a battering ram. Eric went to the Hurlburt house. A million thoughts run through my head. Did he hurt Eric? Or worse . . . did he kill him?

"You want to help me? Tell her to give me the evidence." He turns and yells at Cricket, "Now!"

"I don't know what you are talking about," Cricket whispers.

"I said don't lie to me!" he bellows, pressing the gun against Cricket's head.

"No, please, don't hurt her," I whimper as a sharp pain low in my abdomen blurs my vision.

"She's lying to me! I don't like it when people *lie* to me!"

"I know," I sniff, gripping my stomach. "No . . . no one likes to be lied to, but you have to tell us what you want."

"I want the evidence you have on me," Chris says, pulling the gun from Cricket's head. "I heard that cop and PI talking about it."

"Okay, okay." I nod, unable to hold back the tears as they slide down my face. "You spoke with Eric and Sheriff McKnight? Did you hurt them?"

"Stop *talking* and give me the evidence. I'm getting impatient, and you *don't* want me to do something that will hurt her, do you?" Chris points the gun at Cricket. "Now, tell her to give me the evidence."

"Chris—"

"I'm not Chris!" he lies, pointing the gun at me as another cramp clenches my abdomen.

"O-okay, my m-mistake." I point a shaky finger at Cricket. "She needs to know what evidence you want." It's getting harder to stay calm. This kind of stress can't be good for my baby, and the cramps scare me more than Chris and his gun.

"I want all of it!" He points to the computers with his gun. "Give all of it to me."

"You don't have to do this." Cricket swallows but doesn't move toward the computers. "You'll only make it worse."

"It's already worse! I have to leave the country." He pushes Cricket's chair toward the computers. "I want the hard drive and the laptop."

"Okay." Cricket nods, shutting her laptop lid. "I need to stand so I can pull the hard drive."

Sirens sound in the background, alerting Chris. He keeps his gun on Cricket and goes to the window, pushing the blinds apart. "You called the cops!"

"We didn't call the cops. You've been with us the entire time," I try to assure him as my heart pounds in my ears. "Did you hurt Eric? Or the sheriff?"

"No!" he yells. "I got out of there before they knew I was there."

"That's good." I wince. "I can help you. You haven't done anything serious."

Chris turns to me, his hands on his head. "What am I going to do?"

"I can help you," I whisper, relief easing the tightness in my chest. The sirens blare outside of the office. Eric wasn't hurt, he's safe. I hope I can see him one more time.

"No, no, no . . .." Chris hits his head with his fists. His eyes widen with a desperate fear like a cornered wild animal.

"If you let us go—"

"No!" He points the gun at me, my heart stopping as a cramp tightens my abdomen and unable to hold back a sob, I cry out.

"Please . . . I need to see a doctor," I whisper through my panic.

"No one is going *anywhere*!"

"She's pregnant. You need to *let her go*." Cricket glares at Chris. She stands slowly, holding her hands up. "Let her go, please. I'll stay here, just let her go."

He looks at me and pales. "No."

"I can help you get away," she tries to negotiate.

"How? You have a teleportation machine hiding somewhere?" He holds his hands out wide then points the gun at Cricket's face.

Cricket moves faster than my tear-filled eyes can track, her hands a blur of movement as she disarms Chris of his gun, her elbow cracks his nose, and blood spurts out. I gag at the sight of it, feeling dizzy. Chris covers his nose, blood seeping through his fingers.

"Get down on the ground!" Cricket screams at Chris.

"You broke my nose," he shrieks, not moving.

"I'll break more if you don't get down on the ground. *Now!*" Cricket orders, taking two steps back from him.

Chris holds up two bloody hands and gets down on his knees. "Shoot me," he begs. "My life is over, just shoot me."

"You aren't getting off that easily, but I will shoot you if you don't get down on the ground. I won't kill you, but I *will* hurt you again," Cricket warns. When he gets on the ground, Cricket glances at me. "Sarah, can you walk?"

"I'll get help." I nod, struggling to stand. The cramping has stopped, but I can't breathe. I have to get outside. I have to find Eric.

Expect Forever

24
~Eric~

"We're calling in River Bend PD for assistance," McKnight tells me, his hand clamped down hard on my shoulder. Rage and anger churn in my gut. The call came in not long after one of McKnight's deputies arrived at the Hurlburts' house. He didn't tell me what the call said, only that we need needed to go.

"Don't fucking touch me!" I growl at him, trying to shake off his hand. When we arrived at Sarah's office, it was surrounded by cop cars. McKnight told me Chris Hurlburt is holding Cricket and possibly Sarah hostage. Knowing Sarah is in there rips away my ability to think rationally. "I'm going in there."

"I'm not going to let you do that." He squeezes my shoulder harder.

"How do we know he's in there?" I clench my fist. I don't care if McKnight slaps me with an assault charge, I'll take him out if he stands between Sarah and me.

"Larry is in the office. When he heard screaming, he called the police." McKnight squeezes my shoulder. "Eric, I'm letting you stay here. Don't make me regret this."

"Or what?" I glare at the man I want to hate but the concern in his eyes only puts fear in mine.

"I'll put you in cuff." McKnight releases me and steps in close. "Eric—"

"*Sarah* is in there," I choke out.

"I know," he whispers, staring at me sympathetically. "I know."

"Eric!" Jax's calls from behind the police tape blocking traffic.

McKnight waves Jax in, then looks at me. "Don't me make me regret this." He looks over at Jax. "Keep him behind the perimeter or I'm slapping cuffs on."

"Come on, Eric." Jax tugs on my arm, pulling me away from where McKnight is barking out orders at officers standing by their vehicles, with guns drawn, pointed at Sarah's office.

"I can't stand here and watch." I rip my arm from Jax. I'm carrying my gun, if I slip in through the back door, I can surprise Chris Hurlburt if he's in the conference room or Sarah's office. All I need is one shot and everything will be over. "I need to go around back."

"You're not going anywhere. Let McKnight do his job."

"Do you really think I'm going to sit back and let McKnight and his *protocols* save Sarah? She's in there. Alone. I'm going in." I point at the building.

"Fine, but I'm not letting you go in alone." Jax stands his ground.

Fuck! I scan over the building, running through scenarios, trying to figure out the best way to get around McKnight's deputies. The front door suddenly opens, and Sarah emerges shaken, clenching her lower stomach.

I take off, ignoring McKnight, who yells something at me before I shove him aside. Sarah sees me and her eyes roll as she wobbles on her feet before they give out on her. I catch her before she hits the ground.

"I need an ambulance!" I roar, tilting Sarah's head back.

"Cricket . . . she . . . stopped Chris," Sarah whispers, shaking in my arms. She looks so pale and there is pain in her eyes.

"Shh, don't speak, it's okay." I push the hair from her face, feeling helpless. "Can someone call a damn ambulance!"

McKnight rushes over to us. "Is Chris Hurlburt still in there?"

"Y-yes, Cricket . . . stopped him," Sarah stutters trying to point at the building.

"I need some help in here!" Larry yells from the front door, waving at McKnight.

Paramedics surround me as McKnight rushes into the building. They bring a stretcher and I help them lay Sarah on it. She grabs my hand as her eyes widen when they put an oxygen mask over her mouth and nose. "I'm here."

"Is she okay?" Jax walks beside me as the paramedics push Sarah's stretcher toward the ambulance.

"I don't know," I choke out, not letting go of Sarah's hand.

Jax runs a hand through his hair. "I'll . . . I'll meet you at the hospital."

I don't say anything, I don't look back. I climb into the ambulance, never taking my eyes off Sarah. The rage and anger coursing through me earlier turns into a bone-chilling fear.

"Her blood pressure is high," I hear a paramedic say and I look at him. "How far along is she?"

"Six months," I whisper, placing a hand on her stomach. "We're having a girl. Ericah."

"That's a pretty name," the paramedic tells me, and I think he's trying to reassure me, but it doesn't help.

Sarah pulls the oxygen mask from her face. "Ericah?"

"You need to keep that on." I try to put the mask back, but she pushes my hand away.

"Ericah." Sarah places a hand over mine and looks to the paramedic. "I haven't felt her move."

"The doppler is picking up a strong heartbeat," a paramedic shares running a wand over Sarah's stomach. "You've got a fighter."

"Did . . . did you hear that." Sarah sighs with tears running down the side of her face. "We have a fighter."

"We do," I whisper running a hand over her head and kissing her hand. "Just like her mom."

*****

"The good news is that you didn't go into premature labor, but you gave us a scare," Dr. Cantana tells Sarah before looking up at me. "We want to keep you overnight for observation."

Sarah squeezes my hand. "And our baby?"

"Her heartbeat is strong, her position is right where we want her, but you need to take it easy. We want her to stay put until she's ready to come out."

I smile with relief. "Thank you, doctor."

"You two take care." He pats Sarah's shoulder and leaves us.

Without asking permission, I climb into bed with Sarah, tucking her under my arm. "How do you feel?"

"I'm okay, Eric." Sarah relaxes into my side. "Is Cricket okay?"

"I don't know." I kiss her temple.

Sarah tilts her head up. "You should check on her."

"I don't want to leave you," I say and pull my phone from my pocket. It feels like days have passed, when in reality, it's only been a few hours. I have several missed called and text messages but before I can respond, there is a soft knock on the door.

"Hey," McKnight greets us both. "How are you?"

"I'm fine, Warren, and so is our baby." Sarah smiles and sits up. "How is Cricket?"

"She's good." McKnight rubs his chin. "Colson, you trained her well."

"Trained? What happened?" I demand, getting off the bed, not understanding what he means.

Sarah places a hand on my arm. "She disarmed Chris Hurlburt, stopped him."

"She did *what*?"

"Broke his nose, too," McKnight shares, glancing over his shoulder. "She also said you would be pissed when you found out."

"Damn straight I'm pissed," I cry out. "She could have got herself killed or you—" I turn and look at Sarah.

"Eric," a reluctant Cricket walks into the room, "I knew what I was doing. Griffin has been making me train in self-defense with him for over a year. Please don't be mad."

I take a deep breath and release it, forcing my shoulders to relax. "I'm not mad." I know I sound mad so I soften my tone. "Are you okay?"

"I'm great." Cricket smiles shyly. "We got our guy."

McKnight nods. "He confessed to it all."

"That's fantastic news." Sarah squeezes my arm.

"Yeah," I say, nodding my head.

"You're going to yell at Griffin later, aren't you?" Cricket scrunches her nose while wringing her fingers.

"Absolutely I am." I nod. "Why the hell was he training you? And why didn't you tell me?"

"After Holden took me on a bond enforcement case, Griffin said if I didn't, he would tell you that Holden took me," Cricket confesses, looking guilty.

"I don't see what the big deal is," McKnight chimes in, looking between the two of us. "I think all women should be trained in self-defense."

"Of course, they should," I spit out. "That isn't the problem."

"Then what is?" Sarah asks, watching me with a frown.

"Cricket, you could have been seriously hurt." I pinch the bridge of my nose. "Training in self-defense and disarming a deranged criminal are two very different things." I look at Sarah then back at Cricket. "Thank you."

"Huh?"

"You saved Sarah, and Ericah . . .. I should have thanked you." I run a hand down the back of my head. "I shouldn't have gotten upset. I'm sorry."

"Colson apologizing," McKnight mutters. "Hell must have frozen over."

"I didn't mean to scare you. I was worried, Sarah looked sick, and I saw an opportunity, so I took it." Cricket steps closer to Sarah.

"I know." I come around Sarah's bed and pull Cricket in for a hug. "I'm glad nothing happened. Thank you for saving my family."

"Thank you, Cricket." Sarah smiles from her bed.

"Are you okay?" Cricket asks when I release her, and she walks to Sarah. "They wouldn't tell us anything."

"I'm good and so is Ericah."

"I love the name." Cricket smiles at me. "And I'm so relieved you are okay. I was so scared you were going into labor."

"I was scared I was going into in labor, too," Sarah confesses and McKnight waves me over.

"Do you mind stepping outside?" . McKnight thumbs toward the hall. I follow him out to the hall where a deputy is standing outside the door. He nods at McKnight, then steps away. "What I'm about to tell you is going to piss you off, so I need to know you'll stay calm."

"Okay." I crack my neck, crossing my arms over my chest. Whenever McKnight starts off with a warning, it's usually followed by bad news.

"We had to bring Chris Hurlburt to the hospital to get checked out. He's chained to a bed and I have two deputies on him. Once he's released, we'll book him."

"The *bastard's* here?" I hiss quietly at him then glance at Sarah, who's chatting happily with Cricket.

"I'm placing a deputy outside Sarah's door, so you have nothing to worry about, but I wanted to let you know." McKnight taps my chest. "You won't do anything, will you?"

I shove McKnight's hand away. "I'm not an idiot."

"That's debatable," McKnight says, trying to lighten the mood. "I'm glad Sarah and Ericah are okay."

"Yeah, me too," I breathe out. "I thought I was going to lose them."

"I know." McKnight nods with understanding. "We made a good team."

"That's debatable." I laugh. "Cricket did most of the work."

"True, she's good. I tried to offer her a job."

"Did she laugh in your face?" I smirk, feeling the tension in my shoulders ease up.

"No, but she did call me sweet."

"Sounds about right."

McKnight slaps the back of my shoulder. "You have a lot of people waiting to see you and Sarah. Do you want me to tell them leave?"

"No, they won't leave. Just let me have a little more time with Sarah," I say extending my hand. "For what it's worth, I don't hate you."

McKnight shakes my hand. "I don't hate you, either."

"I still think you're an asshole, though."

"The feeling's mutual. I'll send your family in soon. Take care of your woman."

I wave goodbye to McKnight and go back into Sarah's room. Cricket is quick to tell us goodbye before leaving the room, and I climb back into bed with Sarah.

"Eric." Sarah looks up at me.

"Yeah, Sarah?" I run a finger along her jaw.

"I was so scared," she whispers, and her lips tremble a little. I hate the look of fear in her eyes and vow to never let her feel scared again.

"I know. I wish you didn't have to go through that, but you can't let this get to you, it isn't good for Ericah."

Sarah shifts to her side. "I know but— And I'm not letting it get to me, but what is getting to me . . . is that I haven't told you how I feel."

I brush her hair to the side. "How you feel?"

"I love you, Eric," she says, placing a hand on my face. "I should have told you sooner."

I close my eyes and press my forehead against hers. I've waited a long time to hear her say the words. "Does this mean you'll marry me?"

"Yes." She nods her head with tears in her eyes, and my heart swells with joy.

"Are you kidding me!" Burns cries out at the door.

"We'll let you two have a minute," Miss Janet says, tugging on Burns.

"Not a single one of these jackwagons have gotten down on one knee." Burns scowls at my brothers, who are smirking at us from the hall. Burns then points at Sarah. "Make him ask you again. On. One. Knee."

"Okay," Sarah says covering her smile with a hand then looks up at me and I kiss her.

"Are you really going to make me ask you again?"

"Yes," she smiles, "and I expect you down on one knee."

Thank you

I hope you enjoyed Expect Forever and would appreciate it if you would leave a review. Reviews help readers find my books and keeps me motivated to continue to write.

Acknowledgements

Deepest love and appreciation to my family who support me as I venture down this amazing journey. I love you all so much.

Madelyn you have been a great sounding board, thank you. You are an amazing woman, and I am so very proud of you.

To my husband thank you for your support and encouragement.

Rachael Leissner I'm so lucky to get to work with you. Thank you for everything you do. You are amazing!

The Next Step PR, thank you for promoting my book and providing some much-needed guidance. You ladies are amazing, and I am so happy I was able to work with you all.

Silvia Curry you were a blessing I am so thankful for. You are a genius editor and I look forward to working with you more.

To my readers, thank you for taking the time to read and share my book. I am so grateful to each and every one of you!

About the Author

Amanda Lee Dixon lives in the weather crazed Midwest with her husband, three teenagers and two mouthy malamutes. When she isn't working on the Peak Valley Forever Series, she is obsessively reading romance and fantasy books or pen shopping. Her weaknesses are colorful pens, planners and coffee.

Connection with Amanda:
www.amandaleedixon.com